Theaker's Quarterly Fiction #60

Edited by
Stephen Theaker
and John Greenwood

Theaker's Quarterly Fiction #60

Edited by
Stephen Theaker
and John Greenwood

Cover Artist

Howard Watts

Contributors

Andrew Peters
Douglas J. Ogurek
Douglas Thompson
Jule Owen
Nicki Robson
Rafe McGregor

Contents

Editorial

9   Emergency Questions
Stephen Theaker

Fiction

15   The Lost Testament
Rafe McGregor

25   Turning Point
Nicki Robson

37   Yttrium
Douglas Thompson

53   Amongst the Urlap
Andrew Peters

91   Doggerland
Jule Owen

The Quarterly Review

Reviews by Stephen Theaker, Douglas J. Ogurek, and Rafe McGregor

Books

108   All Systems Red, by Martha Wells (Tor.com)
Stephen Theaker

109   Closet Dreams, by Lisa Tuttle (infinity plus)
Stephen Theaker

110   Final Girls, by Mira Grant (Subterranean Press)
Stephen Theaker

110   Proof of Concept, by Gwyneth Jones (Tor.com)
Stephen Theaker

112   Working for Bigfoot, by Jim Butcher
(Subterranean Press)
Stephen Theaker

Comics

113   I Hate Fairyland, Vol. 1: Madly Ever After, by Skottie
Young (Image Comics)
Stephen Theaker

114   Michael Turner's Soulfire: Omnibus 1, by Michael
Turner, J.T. Krul, Marcus To and chums
(Aspen Comics)
Stephen Theaker

Events

116   Eastercon 2017: Innominate
Stephen Theaker

118   Into the Unknown: a Journey Through Science
Fiction, curated by Patrick Gyger (Barbican)
Stephen Theaker

Films

120   Alien: Covenant, by John Logan and Dante Harper
(Twentieth Century Fox et al.)
Rafe McGregor

123   Guardians of the Galaxy, Vol. 2, by James Gunn
(Marvel Studios)
Stephen Theaker

124   It Comes at Night, by Trey Edward Shults
(A24 et al.)
Douglas J. Ogurek

126   The Mummy, by David Koepp, Christopher
        McQuarrie and Dylan Kussman (Universal
        Pictures et al.)
        Douglas J. Ogurek

128   Pirates of the Caribbean: Dead Men Tell No Tales,
        by Jeff Nathanson (Walt Disney et al.)
        Douglas J. Ogurek

131   Prometheus, by Jon Spaihts and Damon Lindelof
        (Twentieth Century Fox et al.)
        Rafe McGregor

134   Wonder Woman, by Allan Heinberg
        (Warner Bros et al.)
        Douglas J. Ogurek

       Music

136   Humanz (Deluxe), by Gorillaz (Parlophone)
        Stephen Theaker

       Television

138   Iron Fist, Season 1, by Scott Buck and chums
        (Marvel/Netflix)
        Stephen Theaker

141   Legion, Season 1, by Noah Hawley and chums (FX)
        Stephen Theaker

       Notes

144   Also Received, But Not Yet Reviewed
        Notes by Stephen Theaker

147   About TQF

Emergency Questions

Stephen Theaker

Not a lot on my mind this time, so here are my answers to some *Emergency Questions* taken from the Richard Herring book of that name. I hope it gives you some insight into the thought that goes into this zine.

If you had to would you give up chocolate or cheese?
Chocolate.

Which is the best pie?
Steak and ale pie.

What is the most unlikely thing you've done on a bus?
A burly bloke attacked a bus driver and I ran to help. Then, realising that if the guy punched me even once it would probably kill me, I contented myself with shouting "Hey, stop that!" while jumping back and forth and tugging at his jacket. I think it helped.

Have you ever been somewhere foreign and obscure and bumped into someone you know?
Yes, when I arrived in France for the third year of my French degree, a chap I knew from school was there. It was very awkward. The sole of my shoe broke off and I had to go and get some superglue to fix it.

What is the worst Adam Sandler film?
Of those I've seen, which is most of them, *Bulletproof*.

Harder to choose the best but it's probably *The Wedding Singer* or *Jack and Jill*.

How do you sleep at night?
I read for between five minutes and two hours depending on what time I go to bed, put my Kindle or Kobo down, and then wake up an hour later wondering where my reading device has gone and why there are terrifying visions looming over the bed. You get used to it.

What's the most pretentious book you've ever bought, but never read?
I've a whole shelf of Folio Society history and poetry books and I've never read any of them. I liked the idea of owning books with golden text on the spines.

When you are asked to imagine a time or place when you are calm and happy, what time and/or place do you imagine?
Reading the *Hellblazer* collection *Original Sins* in an armchair with a cup of tea and a packet of Hobnobs. That's still the ideal.

Do you remember Barnaby the Bear?
Yes, he was on the cover of what I think was the first comic we had delivered weekly from the newsagent, *Pippin in Playland*. Wasn't long before we were getting comics through the door practically every day, with I think three on Thursday!

What's your worst experience with the delivery company Yodel?
They were delivering a bookcase. The cardboard was wet and green and the bits of the bookcase were bulging through. "Sorry, what's happened to this?" I asked. "Don't worry about it," said the driver, "that's just water from the flowers."

Have you ever been in a canoe?
No, just a rowing boat.

What's in issue 60 of Theaker's Quarterly Fiction?
Thanks for asking, Rich! We have terrific stories by
Rafe McGregor, Nicki Robson, Douglas Thompson,
Andrew Peters and Jule Owen, that will take you on a
dizzying ride from the nineteenth century to the
distant future, plus nineteen reviews by Douglas
Ogurek, Rafe McGregor and me.

**Is there anything new to tell readers about the
@TheakersQrtly Twitter account?**
Why yes, thanks for reminding me! Last year I read
three hundred books but only reviewed thirty or forty
of them. I've started writing one-tweet reviews on our
Twitter account, in order to: 1. Bridge that gap. 2. Stop
myself adding too many reviews to my writing to-do
list. 3. Stop myself from putting off books or films or
audios just because they're the kind of thing that'd be
good to review and I don't have time to review them.
4. Give a nod more often to the kind of things that
aren't always the most convenient to review: ongoing
comics, podcasts, later books in series, that kind of
thing. Follow us if you don't already!

**Is it okay to review books without mentioning the
author?**
Yes, because you're reviewing the book not the person.
I would even *recommend* it if you hated the book.
There's very little you can say about an author in a bad
review that they won't take extremely personally.

**Should a self-publisher pay someone to edit their
book?**
The consensus forming around this is that they
should, but I'm a bit uncomfortable with this industry
growing up around self-published writers. How many
self-published books will sell enough copies to repay
that investment? Editors must be careful not to exploit
amateur writers, or they could find themselves classed
with the vanity presses. If a self-published writer

chooses to spend extra money on a professional edit, fair enough: they may see it as an investment, or if they are hobbyists they may just be happy to spend money on their hobby. But when freelance editors push the line that it's *essential*, there's an element of turkey farmers voting for Christmas.

Did you ever see a leaflet from a company called Captain Pizza and come up with a whole theme song to the tune of "Joxer the Mighty" before realising that it was actually Caspian Pizza?
Yes, that happened to me at the end of June. The lyrics to the song were as follows: "Captain Pizza / Ready to feed ya / He's never stopping / Got all the toppings / He is sailing on a sea / Of cheese and peppero-oni."

Would you prefer to sell 500 copies of a book and lose £1,000, or sell 50 copies and make a profit?
Personally, I would prefer to sell 50 copies and make a profit, and that's because I know that if I lost a thousand pounds on every book I wrote I would not bother to write many more. I posted a survey about this on Twitter and 40% chose the first option, 60% chose the second. But only five votes were cast so the results cannot be considered conclusive.

Should we look out for the new issues of Interzone?
Yes, please do: issue 271 includes my review of *Ex Libris: Stories of Librarians, Libraries and Lore*, edited by Paula Guran and published by Prime Books, while issue 272 will include my review of *Too Like the Lightning* by Ada Palmer, which might seem a bit redundant when it's already been nominated for the Hugo, but it only just came out in the UK.

Were you shocked to discover that a YouTube reviewer had been paid by a major publishing house to review a book?

Yes. I noticed a conversation on Goodreads, where a YouTube reviewer said: "As someone who was paid by Harper to review the book, our contract, as well as the majority of contracts with publishers, explicitly states that Harper cannot influence our thoughts in any way." They are giving you money to review their book! How can that not affect your thoughts? The book in question showed how vulnerable such a set-up leaves a young reviewer. The book had been criticised for its portrayal of race, and the YouTuber faced accusations that she had not mentioned this for financial reasons. We've seen this before, with bloggers being paid to cover certain books. For the sake of a little bit of money, they lose respect and their reputations, become a joke among their peers, while the publishers move on to a new generation of youngsters ready to make the same mistakes in a new medium.

Is it okay to give a book a low rating on Goodreads (or anywhere else) without saying why?
Of course. I spoke with a chap on Twitter who had said that "People who 1-star books on Goodreads with no review deserve eternal nut-kicking in the afterlife." I couldn't disagree more. There's no obligation on readers to explain their thinking. They are not tutors marking an essay. They don't need to give feedback, to help authors do better next time. Most Goodreads users aren't reviewers or writers, they're readers keeping track of their books. You don't have to be able to write a book review for your rating to be valid. I had a similar conversation with a friend who has started a small press and was alarmed to find a slightly negative comment about a book on one of her Facebook posts. The book had been given away for free, the publisher stating: "All feedback gratefully received." However, the feedback received was mildly negative. The publisher said, "To me, that person is a troll", it was a "deliberate

nasty comment", and her first reaction was "stupid woman – if you can't say anything nice, why say anything at all". In a public thread asking for advice, all but one of the respondents advised against deleting it. One said: "I think the main problem with negative feedback ... is that it makes the person on the receiving end feel upset, and that unless it's a constructive criticism ... it's not particularly helpful to just say 'I don't like this'. It also shows that they don't have any real critical skills." This might make perfect sense within a writing circle or a classroom, but readers aren't part of your writing circle. They're customers, not beta readers. Telling writers this kind of thing sets them at odds with an audience that will rarely comply with such expectations. Better to be glad anyone is reading the book at all. If you go to war with your readers, delete their comments, slate them online, or call them names, don't expect them to have much time for your books in future. Out of the billions of people in the world they were one of the very few willing to give your work one chance. They might well have given it another.

I thought there wasn't much on your mind?
I guess I was wrong! It's not uncommon.

Were those last ten questions really in Richard Herring's bestselling book *Emergency Questions*?
No. Most of his were very rude. They might be more suitable for Douglas to answer in his editorial for the forthcoming *Unsplatterpunk 2*, or as I hope he can be persuaded to call it, *Unspla2erpunk*.

Stephen Theaker is the co-editor of Theaker's Quarterly Fiction. His reviews, interviews and articles have appeared in Interzone, Black Static, Prism and the BFS Journal.

The Lost Testament
An Intermezzo

Rafe McGregor

I

"Stop that damned scribbling!"

I looked up from my bedroll to see the little captain framed in the doorway of the block-house. His face was streaked with gunpowder. I could hear and smell the renewed battle raging in the night beyond the threshold.

Tomlinson brandished his service revolver in his fist. Mine was still tucked into his belt. "Stand up! Stop your bloody malingering and show some backbone."

I set my pencil and journal down and struggled to my feet, my head pounding from the blows received during the day. "Am I no longer under arrest?"

"Don't bother me with that nonsense now. The attack is failing. I require you to guide us to the fort by the route you took. Get a move on, man!" He turned and disappeared into the darkness.

I stumbled after him. There was no point in reminding him that I had been unconscious when captured and that I had returned via a path made by a boulder. I emerged into the jungle, the stench of smoke strong in my nostrils and flashes of musket and rifle fire flaring all around. Tomlinson had not only attacked the wrong village, but decided to press the assault home after dusk. While our Goorkhas were more than a match for the Lushai in daylight, every British officer knew that night-time operations were suicide. I made out Tomlinson's pith helmet in the moonlight, bobbing through the bamboo, creepers, and orchids. The fear and focus that combat brings took hold of me and the hammering in my head ceased. I caught up with him.

"Where's Gurung?"

"Who!"

"My *havildar* – where is he?"

He ignored my question. "It's a shambles. The fort has more stone shoots and *panji*-pits than I've ever seen. We've lost two-score men. My *havildar* is out of it. So are three of my *naiks*."

I was shocked. Our fighting strength was a single company of Goorkhas and a tiny troop of half a dozen sappers. I knew exactly why the hilltop fort was being defended with such vigour. When I had tried to warn Tomlinson, he had confined me to the block-house under guard. As we continued our traverse of the steep slope, I heard a man screaming from above, somewhere off to the right. When I returned my attention to Tomlinson, I nearly tripped over the legs of Limbu, one of my men. He was sitting on the ground, propped up against a clump of bamboo, half of his face missing. The fact that I could recognise what was left of him made me realise it was too light. There was also too much smoke. The muzzle flashes were an insufficient cause of the sooty mist thickening around us. I stopped and listened. Somewhere in the middle distance, I could hear a crackling sound that was lower than the retort of the firearms, but constant. Then something else occurred to me.

I caught up with Tomlinson and patted him on the shoulder. "Captain, where are we going?"

He didn't slow down. "What?"

"You said you wanted me to show you the way. Where are we going?"

He darted uphill and I followed, keeping my hands high to protect my eyes from the leaves and branches. "Captain!"

He continued his charge through the brush. A few seconds later we reached what looked like a small *joom*. There were two Goorkhas in cover behind tree trunks, one on either side of the clearing, both scouring the slope for signs of the enemy.

Tomlinson stopped. "Here! We're here!"

"Where?"

"The stone-shoot. Where you were taken prisoner."

"Are you sure it's the same one?"

Tomlinson turned to me, opened his mouth to speak, and froze. His shoulders started to shake and I thought he was going to sob. In the clearing, I could see smoke rolling downwards and a glow from above. The Lushai had taken advantage of the mountain breeze and set fire to the jungle. They were going to burn us off the hill. Tomlinson regained limited control of himself and closed his mouth.

I turned away and bellowed, *"Ayo Gorkhali, ayo Gorkhali!"*

The closest Goorkha heard and ran over to me. His name was Pun, from my half-company. My Nepalese and his English were works in progress so I took care to make my meaning clear. "Gurung, *Havildar* Gurung, find him." I pointed to the right, the way we had come. He nodded and dashed off into the night. I ran to the other man, gave him the same instruction, and sent him in the other direction.

Tomlinson had followed, but was still lost for words. "You see what they're doing, don't you?"

"What! What! Tell me what!" His skin was grey underneath the streaks of dirt. He had no idea what he was doing, let alone the Lushai.

"They've set the jungle alight. The wind is blowing the flames towards us. They'll burn us out and follow behind to finish off the survivors. This isn't a defeat – it's a massacre."

II

Tomlinson and I stood in the small clearing, two Englishmen halfway up a hill in a burning jungle five thousand miles from home. I think he knew then that he was going to die on the North-East Frontier and that none of his white skin, Queen's commission, or two revolvers were going to stop the Lushai from burning, shooting, or stabbing him to death and taking his head as a trophy.

He stamped his foot – once, twice – trying to put a stop to the trembling. "It's your fault, Langham. It's your fault we're in this mess. This mess. *Your* mess."

I closed my eyes and concentrated on the sounds of battle... the crackle and roar of the fire, the occasional crack of a firearm, cries of pain.

"Your orders were simple: take a half-company and raze the village. You couldn't manage it, got yourself captured, put the wind up the n—s, and..." he tailed off.

There is nothing more disgusting than an officer who fails to recognise the humanity of the men under his command, whatever their colour or creed. I opened my eyes in order to express my contempt, but immediately noticed movement to the right. Two figures, gliding through the jungle in silence.

I pointed. "Pun's brought..."

But Pun hadn't brought Gurung back.

There were three men, not two, all short and clean-shaven. The chief wore a cane helmet with a bearskin crest and carried a musket. The warriors wore their long hair in top-knots; one carried a bamboo spear and a buffalo hide shield, the other a musket.

We turned to face them: the chief knelt, the first warrior drew back his spear, and the second fired his musket from the hip. The ball thumped into my right shoulder, the impact spinning me around. I staggered, started to slump, regained my balance. Tomlinson fired his revolver. The round penetrated the first warrior's shield and bowled him over backwards. Tomlinson fired again, hitting the second warrior in the arm. The chief fired his musket at Tomlinson, but the falling flint failed to ignite the powder in the pan. The damp. Tomlinson turned the revolver on him and fired for the third time.

Click!

Tomlinson had failed to count his rounds. The chief dropped the musket and reached for the *dao* at his waist. Tomlinson dropped his Beaumont-Adams and reached for mine in his belt.

I was quicker.

I removed the revolver from his belt with my left hand, placed it against his right temple, and blew the top of his head off.

"Vanhela!"

The chief, Keeper of the Migo and my jailer for the afternoon, halted. He lowered his *dao*.

"I am in command now. We will leave your village in peace."

Vanhela pointed to Tomlinson and asked in his perfect English, "May I take his head?"

"No. If I take a mutilated corpse back to Cachar there will be reprisals. As it stands, I can probably prevent my superiors from finding this place – for a while at least."

Vanhela was joined by the wounded warrior, bleeding but unbowed, *dao* at the ready. The chief snapped a sharp command and the man sheathed his weapon. Vanhela pointed to the other warrior, shot through the throat and in his death throes. "Must I take his head?"

"No. I will order the retreat and you can retrieve your dead. When you hear the signal, douse your fires."

We heard movement through the brush, in the same direction from which Vanhela had come. He nodded to me, turned, and trotted over to retrieve his musket. Then he and his man vanished into the jungle.

Pun, Gurung, and Paim appeared.

Gurung took one look at Tomlinson's corpse, then approached me and said, "What are your orders, *saheb*?"

Pun strode over to the remaining Lushai and bayoneted him through the heart.

"Sound retire. Company is to fall back to this position, removing all our wounded and dead."

"Yes, *saheb*." He nodded to Paim, who put his lips to his bugle.

Gurung and Paim returned to the darkness from whence they had come and Pun waited with me. He cut a bandage from the rolls of the Lushai's cotton sheet and dressed my wound. Then he cut us both kerchiefs to cover our mouths and noses as the smoke intensified.

A few minutes later I heard movement from the left and the first of my men reached us; two carrying the body of a third between them. The sound of gunfire died down, replaced by guttural commands bawled over the crackling of the flames.

III

The Goorkhas rallied to my position with characteristic courage and skill. I established a perimeter in the clearing and the orderlies arrived to tend the wounded. Of the hundred and fourteen Goorkhas and sappers that were now under my command, eighteen had been killed and forty-four wounded over the course of the afternoon and evening. There were six men, five Goorkhas and one sapper, missing in action – which meant that their headless bodies were lying somewhere on the hillside. It was a casualty rate of nearly two-thirds and although I was appalled by the loss, and the poor decision-making on Tomlinson's part that had placed us in this position, I knew it was a small price to pay. I had seen the Migo in its prison and if Vanhela had told me the truth, then he and his band of warriors were all that protected the world from the thing they called the crawling chaos. By nine o'clock the flames had died down and by eleven o'clock the pouring rain had dampened the smoke. I was with the rear-guard when it withdrew at midnight.

When all but the six missing soldiers were reunited with the coolies and mahouts, I ordered a night march to the location of our previous camp so that there would be no dead bodies buried on Vanhela's hill and no reason to return to the prison he guarded with such selfless vigilance.

After a full twenty-four hours of rest, we limped back to Cachar. By the time we reached the safety of the town, a third of the wounded had died. My shoulder was infected and I was delirious with disease, which did away with the need for me to provide a fabrication of either the disaster which had occurred

or the disaster which had been averted. I was
evacuated first to Chittagong and thence to Calcutta.

IV

I remember nothing of my confinement in Calcutta
except that the hospital was crawling with cats. I
became obsessed with the irony that the only man I
had ever killed was an Englishman. Little did I know
that the next man I would kill, thirteen years later,
would also be an Englishman.

V

The Daphla Expedition brought honours and
promotion to several, but for me it held nothing but
misfortune and disaster. For months my life was
despaired of and when at last I came to myself and
became convalescent, I was so weak and emaciated
that a medical board determined not a day should be
lost in sending me back to England. I was dispatched,
accordingly, in the troopship *Serapis* and landed a
month later on Portsmouth jetty, with my health
utterly ruined, but with permission from a paternal
government to spend the next nine months in
attempting to improve it.

I had neither kith nor kin in England and was
therefore as free as air – or as free as an income of
eleven shillings and sixpence a day will permit a man
to be. Under such circumstances, I naturally gravitated
to London, that great cesspool into which all the
loungers and idlers of the Empire are irresistibly
drained. There I stayed for some time at a private hotel
in Craven Street, leading a comfortless, meaningless
existence and spending such money as I had
considerably more freely than I ought. So alarming did

the state of my finances become that I soon realised I must either leave the metropolis and rusticate somewhere in the country or that I must make a complete alteration in my style of living. Choosing the latter alternative, I began by making up my mind to leave the army and to take up employment that would facilitate the continuation of my domicile in the metropolis.

On the very day that I had come to this conclusion, I was descending the stairs to The Dive in Scott's when I heard my name called and, turning round, recognised Fordstam, who had been with me in the Upper Shell at Westminster. The sight of a friendly face in the great wilderness of London is a pleasant thing indeed to a lonely man. In the old days Fordstam had never been a particular crony of mine, but now I hailed him with enthusiasm and he, in his turn, appeared to be delighted to see me. In the exuberance of my joy, I asked him to lunch with me at the Albion and we started off together in a hansom.

"Whatever have you been doing with yourself, Langham?" he asked in undisguised wonder as we rattled through the crowded London streets. "You are as thin as a lath and as brown as a nut."

I gave him a short sketch of my misadventures and had hardly concluded it by the time we reached our destination.

"Poor devil!" he said, pityingly, after he had listened to my tale. "What are you up to now?"

"Looking for employment," I answered. "Trying to solve the problem as to whether it is possible to find a respectable occupation for a reasonable salary."

"That's a strange thing," remarked my companion, "you are the second man today that has used that expression to me."

"And who was the first?"

"A fellow who is working for the Metropolitan Police Force."

"The police force," I said, "I had not considered a career in the police force."

"Many of its officers are former military men, including the commissioner, who was a colonel of engineers."

"How could I meet this friend of yours?"

"If you like we shall drive round together after luncheon..."

Rafe McGregor *is the author of The Value of Literature, The Architect of Murder, five collections of short fiction, and over one hundred magazine articles, journal papers, and review essays. He lectures at the University of York and can be found online at https://twitter.com/rafemcgregor.*

Turning Point

Nicki Robson

Every great mistake has a halfway moment, a split
second when it can be recalled and perhaps remedied.
– Pearl S. Buck

The pub had filled up since the end of the quiz. Not
for the first time, Jake thought it funny that the very
thing designed to pull punters in actually succeeded in
keeping them away. Maybe word had got out about the
competitiveness. The air had definitely turned blue a
few times tonight.

He pushed his way to the bar, the dregs of his last
pint still clutched in one hand. He drained the glass
while he waited for the barman to hand change to a
young woman who was dressed more for a club than a
pub. She gathered up the three drinks she had been
served and turned to push her way through the crowd.
Jake twisted himself sideways to let her pass.

"Gonna try and nick her next are yeh? Like yeh did
first prize?"

Jake squinted at the man who'd spoken. His gaze
slid down to the tattoos around the man's throat.

Snips and snails and puppy-dogs' tails...

"Nah, she's all yours, mate."

The tattooed man stared at him as though he'd
expected a different answer, muttered something and
turned away.

"Same again?" the barman asked, one eyebrow
cocked.

Jake groaned. "Always a bad sign when the new staff

learns your order before your name," he managed to say although he noticed that his words were starting to slur and mingle.

After a few minutes, he made his way back with a tray of pint glasses. The table had been cleared of everything but disintegrating beermats. Mikey, Brad and Tom picked off their own drinks.

I can't be that *drunk,* he thought. The tray seemed steady enough.

"But *why* would it happen?" Mikey said once they were settled again.

"Why what? Eh?" Jake looked around at the others. He had obviously returned in the middle of a conversation.

"Why *does* your life flash before your eyes when you die?" Tom said.

Silence fell around the table as the weight of the issue settled on them. Brad was the first to rouse himself.

"It's a 'red book' thing innit?" he said.

The others looked at him. He stared back, unfazed.

"It's obvious. That programme that was on when we was little..."

"*This Is Your Life,*" Mikey said, nodding. "Michael Parkinson."

Silence again. Frowns spread across faces.

"Nah, it wasn't him, it was the guy who did the antiques thing," Jake said. "My nan never missed it."

"Yeah, well anyway," Brad went on, "it's a look back on your life, just before you peg it. Gives you a chance to see what you've done."

"But what's the point?" Mikey said. "It's too late to do anything about it then."

They fell silent. Jake shrugged and supped his pint. Mikey thought most things were pointless and after another couple of beers he'd be saying it was a waste of time breathing.

Around them the crowds began to thin. They were almost at the bottom of their drinks when the "time" bell rang. When Brad said, "sup up" and prepared for a final trip to the bar, the pub was almost empty. Only a few small clusters remained. One, Jake noticed, was the group they had "pipped" in the tie-breaker to win the quiz (turned out he'd known the width of The Last Supper). In the dim light, the tattoos seemed to crawl round the man's throat.

That's the beer, mate.

By kicking out time it was just the two quiz teams left.

"Your taxi's here," the barman told Brad as he cleared the last of their glasses.

For a moment, Jake wondered how he knew it was for Brad. Surely the landlord had not told him every little habit of the regular patrons?

"Right," Brad said, "I'll just take a piss an' I'll be right out."

"Sounds like a plan." Jake followed him.

When they returned to the bar Mikey and Tom had gone. The barman was waiting to lock the door behind them.

"OK, OK, we'll take the hint," Brad said, grinning.

The barman held out Brad's jacket as they passed.

"Go carefully, lads," he said.

A shiver ran down Jake's spine.

Chilly outside, he thought. Still, his skin felt clammy.

"I'll see you, Jake," Brad said with a wave.

Jake watched his friend climb into the back seat of the taxi and wished, for the first time he could remember, that he was travelling in the same direction.

He turned to head home, shrugging his coat closer around his throat and just in time to see something flash towards his face.

He realised that he was on the ground, and that the middle of his face (he wasn't convinced his nose was still there) was a mass of pain but the reason escaped him. For a second he thought that he had walked into something.

Yeah, a fist.

Jake peered around but his eyes were watering, causing the too-bright street lamps to blur together.

Something slammed into his right thigh, sending a burst of pain shooting down towards his knee and up towards his kidney. He felt sick.

Shit! Move!

He rolled to his left, trying to use his good leg to push himself away from the attack. His senses started to return and he realised that they were all around him, getting ready.

Jake sagged down and pulled his legs up – *going foetal* – and waited for the inevitable.

Seconds later he was still waiting.

What are they…?

He risked looking out from under his arm. Figures surrounded him still and looked distinctly… *statuesque.* He uncurled a little then tensed again but the attack did not resume. Finally, he sat up in one quick motion.

The quiz rivals stood within kicking distance. The tattooed man had a fist raised, ready to smash it down, while two others each had a foot drawn back to target head and spine simultaneously.

Nice, Jake thought to himself.

He stepped out of the frozen circle and looked around. The rest of the street was already still, there was nothing that would reveal if more than his attackers were frozen.

Brad?

Jake looked towards the end of the street where Brad's taxi had stopped in mid-turn. He could see the red tail lights and he ran towards them, amazed that his leg could take it.

"Brad!" he shouted. His voice was thick with phlegm. He hawked and spat a globule into the gutter.

The taxi waited for him.

What's the point?

Even if he could open the door (and he was prepared to bet that he couldn't) his friend would be immobile inside.

He reached for the handle anyway and pulled. It swung open. Jake stepped back, no longer sure that he wanted his friend to get out.

A dark head emerged, then a leg, shoulders and a body. Jake found himself looking at Bradley Fisher but it was not his friend, Brad. The imposter stared into the middle-distance as though he was a robot awaiting instruction.

"Brad?" Jake said, out of hope rather than expectation.

At the sound of his name, Brad seemed to come to life. His posture softened and he looked at Jake and almost seemed to recognise him.

"It's not really you, is it?" Jake said, half to himself.

"No, not really," Brad admitted and grinned.

Jake shivered. He'd heard that voice before, but where?

"OK. But you got out of the taxi even though everything else is frozen..." He looked back along the street to where his attackers waited. From this position, he saw that they were arranged around a pool of light from the nearest streetlamp. The whole street looked like a film set or a stage.

"Can you help me?" Jake asked, turning his attention back to the man who was not-Brad.

"I can try."

Not-Brad strode back along the street towards the pub and Jake found himself trotting to keep up. He had no idea what not-Brad could do but he seemed to have a purpose.

On reaching the four attackers not-Brad stopped and resumed his "waiting" posture.

Shit! Apparently, his purpose had been to cross the distance as quickly and efficiently as possible without running. *Great!*

Jake circled not-Brad. He half expected to be able to peer in one ear and see some little creature twisting knobs and pulling levers to operate him like some giant machine. Perhaps he was voice activated.

And perhaps I'm already dead.

Jake looked around at the tableau again feeling as though there should be something there that would unlock the mystery. If only he could see it – and recognise it.

What's wrong with this picture?

He realised that the phrase had been running through his head since he had pushed himself up off the floor.

"Is this something to do with my life flashing before my eyes?" he said.

Not-Brad looked round, twisting from the waist to do so and causing his arms to lift away from his side.

"Nothing seems to be 'flashing' here," not-Brad said.

Jake looked closer. He was sure he had heard a note of amusement in his friend's tone.

Except it's not Brad, he reminded himself, *they don't even have the same accent.*

"They were attacking me," Jake told him. "I knew I was going to die and then everything stopped..."

"I see that," not-Brad said.

"But you don't know why?"

"No," not-Brad admitted.

And yet you're here, whoever you are, moving and talking to me about what happened.

"Can you think of any way for me to get out of this?" Jake said, gesturing to his attackers.

Not-Brad tilted his head to one side to consider. "Not really," he said at length.

Jake threw his hands up and laughed. "Great, so I'm having a pointless conversation with a possessed friend. There's nothing I can do except wait for the world to start turning again."

"That would appear to be correct," not-Brad said and resumed his waiting pose.

Jake covered his face with his hands but only succeeded in sending spikes of pain through his nose and cheekbones.

Pain means I'm still alive.

"Maybe this is a turning point," Jake said at last. "Maybe this is my chance to look at the situation – objectively, if you like – and work out what I need to do differently."

He spoke out loud but his rhetoric was entirely for his own benefit.

"I think that the turning point was in there," not-Brad said, one arm shooting out to point at the pub and almost delivering another blow to Jake's mashed nose, "a tie-break ago."

Jake stared at his not-friend. He sounded more like Mikey than Brad and not much help either way.

"Well, pardon me for disagreeing with you," Jake said, "but there must be a reason why this is happening."

Maybe if I could attract someone's attention, he thought, turning his focus towards the houses in the street. But would they respond? If everyone else is frozen...

Except not-Brad.

"Ha!" Jake whirled round to face not-Brad. "It's not about changing things *now,* it's about changing things when everything starts moving again."

He turned back to the houses, a row of terraces that opened directly onto the street, and walked along in front of them. At the third house, he found what he was looking for.

The curtains had been cracked open and a woman peered through. Like the others, she was frozen, but she had heard the commotion and had come to the window to look out. She was small and slim enough to be called petite but she did not need to come out and take on his attackers... she just had to call the police.

All I need to do is get over here and show her that I'm human and I need help.

He tried looking over her head but could see nothing. The room seemed dark... no that was wrong... the light was on... so what was blocking his view? He looked up and then jerked back as he realised the woman's partner had followed her to the window. He might not be close enough to see what was happening outside but he was close enough for Jake to see that he was over six feet tall.

"Now that's the kind of ally I need," he muttered to himself.

"If you think so."

Jake jumped. He swung round, staggering sideways and thudding into the window with one shoulder. Not-Brad had crossed to stand behind him.

"I have to go now," not-Brad said and began to walk back towards his taxi.

Jake's heart leapt. He wanted to shout after his not-friend, to beg him to come back, but he knew that it was futile. Not-Brad's last comment carried such doubt that Jake's knees felt weak, his whole body seemed to slouch down.

I have a choice, he told himself. *It looked like Brad but it sounded like Mikey and Mikey would say it was "game over". Brad wouldn't think that, he'd want me to get to that window and get help.*

When he looked at the window again he found that he had to peer upwards and across a great distance. Somehow, he had staggered back to the middle of the road and his sagging knees had brought him close to the asphalt again.

It's time.

The words were not his but he knew that they were true. He was back in the circle again and his muscles were contracting to draw him into his foetal position.

But it's not over, he told himself. *I have a choice.*

The pain in his nose and thigh seemed to intensify as he came back to reality. In a second the world would unfreeze and he had to be ready to move.

What's wrong with this picture?

The phrase came to his mind unbidden.

No, that part's gone. We're moving again...

Three blows landed simultaneously. The one to his head, though glancing, set his ears ringing while lights danced in front of his eyes.

Shit! Move!

He had intended to move before the drawn-back limbs were propelled forward but he had allowed himself to be distracted. Now he pushed aside all pain and gathered himself, ready to launch upwards.

His movement, swift and powerful, took himself and his attackers by surprise. His upward thrust lifted his feet off the ground and caused the four men to fall back.

Now run!

He hurled himself across the street, aiming for the secret witnesses, to show them his human, bloodied face. The curtains were closed.

Jake whirled round and leaned heavily against the window.

What happened?

As he took in the scene – his attackers righting themselves and beginning a slow advance towards him

– he realised his mistake. He had run the wrong way. The witnesses were across the other side. The window behind him was dark; he should have registered that...

I was preoccupied!

His attackers came on, fists and teeth clenched. Jake pushed himself upright and tried to ready himself as best he could. Then, beyond the enclosing circle, on the other side of the street, a front door started to open.

Yes! Thank you!

Jake tried to shout the words but they stuck in his throat. He expected his attackers to turn as the door swung ever wider but they seemed frozen in place.

Again?

Jake tried to step forward to greet his saviour, half expecting not-Brad to emerge through the doorway, but his own limbs were frozen. He could only watch.

The man that Jake had seen through the window stepped out into the street and looked around, frowning. His height was closer to seven feet than six and his dark skin was pulled tight over bulging muscles. Beside him, the petite blonde woman was as different as it was possible to be. While the big man twisted and turned to take in the scene his not-partner assumed a waiting posture.

"Look they've got him cornered," the man said, starting forward towards Jake's attackers. "I can take them."

The woman followed behind him. "What if they have knives?"

It wasn't a woman's voice. She sounded like a man. She sounded like the *barman!* If Jake had been capable of turning his head he would have glared accusingly at the pub.

"They would have used them already," the big man said but he sounded uncertain.

Jake focused on the him. He could no longer bring

himself to use the word "saviour". The man wore flip-flops with his jogging trousers and vest top, the gold chain around his neck was fine not chunky and his fingernails looked as though they had been manicured earlier that day.

You're no fighter, Jake thought, *probably an insurance salesman.*

Jake would have laughed at the idea if he could have. It would have been a hollow laugh that would have ended in a sob but even that seemed to be beyond his capability.

"Look, he's crying," the man said.

"Of course he is, he's going to die," the not-wife said.

Jake imagined goosebumps spreading over his skin.

"You're not my wife. She wouldn't say such a thing." As the man said it, he had to turn to shout it across the street. She had almost reached their front door. Soon he followed her and they disappeared inside. The door closed part way and stopped. Then everything else started moving again.

Jake's gaze remained fixed on the door. After two more steps his attackers turned to see what he was looking at. Finally, the door clicked closed again, he heard the key turn in the lock.

No! Don't listen to her!

Jake's attackers turned towards him again, each grinning as his last hope of help was dashed.

"It's just you, then," one of them said, flexing his fingers before curling both hands into fists.

He could not hope for another "turning point", another frozen moment to reassess.

We're still in the same one, he told himself. *The decision's been made.*

He lowered his head and looked up at them from under a furrowed brow.

"Looks that way," he said, and charged.

Nicki Robson writes fantasy and horror fiction. She has had short stories placed in competitions run by the British Fantasy Society and others published in anthologies from Twilight Tales in the US. She is based in Yorkshire and is currently working on a YA fantasy novel.

Yttrium

Part One

Douglas Thompson

The day I killed myself, all my real troubles started. I was a duplinaut on Yttria. Now, if you don't know what that first term means, or that the second term is a nickname for a planet fourteen light years from Earth, then that must mean you're from the distant past or future or that you're not human. Either way, I can't help you. But wait. Maybe I can. Perhaps this story has a significance bigger than its characters and its setting. I guess only the process of telling will reveal that, so I better just start.

I was depressed that day. I suppose all our spirits had taken a dive since the fateful transmission of two months beforehand, warning us that a major terrorist attack was endangering the NASA telepedrome headquarters in Nevada. A few hours later we saw and heard an explosion in the background of the live transmission then everything went blank. It's hard to explain how we all reacted. Headless chickens would be the obvious analogy, though that is usually taken to imply lots of strutting and spraying of blood. Zombies would be a better description, the walking dead. There were various buttons and screens to pointlessly paw for the ensuing ten minutes of disbelief, but the horrific truth was staring the five of us in the face like a black hole at the centre of a galaxy. Earth was gone.

Or at least the multi-billion dollar technology back on earth that linked them to us, and provided us with our only possible means of returning home.

When Ellie, our operational commander, eventually gave up and sat down to stare off vacantly into space, we pretty much all followed suit. Except that it wasn't space, we were each left gazing out one window or another at the surface of Yttria, a grey apparently barren planet of mountain ranges as jaggedly serrated as something drawn by the map-making hand of J.R.R. Tolkien on acid. I can still remember Ellie's face at that moment, how she looked back then, blonde hair, jet-black survival suit. She would change, in my eyes, even in the ensuing months, not just because of the stress and the hardship, but because I would fall in love with her. Love, that stupid old piece of human pipesmoke, all pheromones and hormones. We can analyse it and deconstruct it, but we can't get above it. Not yet anyway. I suppose the same could be said about thirst or hunger, but we should be able to live without love more easily, like wolves or other pack animals back in Earth can seem to manage. Bad design somewhere down the line. But I'm digressing.

Five of us left on Yttria alone. Two women, three men, you see, you get the problem? We were just supposed to be visitors, inspectors, not pioneers or settlers. But suddenly all that was going to change. And although I'd always thought of 5 as my lucky number since I was a kid, I see now that it was bad arithmetic for our situation. I would fall in love with Ellie Windcote, despite all my best efforts not to (does rationale have anything to do with that stuff?), but she would fall for Kurt Arnott, who would in turn have a bit of a thing for Valerie Fornara, who would unfortunately quickly forge a fairly workable relationship with Arturo Akamatsu. So I would be left out. Not immediately of course, which might have been bearable, but oh no, human biology is far too tyrannical and humiliating for that. I would find myself the single and rejected one only after two months of doubt and turbulence and embarrassment, awkward scenes and tumultuous feelings, despite all my best efforts to remain a calm highly-trained scientific astronaut. The irony. I joined the duplinaut programme to escape precisely that kind of human monkey business, to be something bigger and better than an animal, and there I was at last a victim of it at its worst. We all remember this sort of stuff, I think, from our teenage years. It's bad enough on Earth. But experiencing all that while fighting for your life on a serrated grey planet infested with glowing crabworms is well beyond endurance. So one afternoon I climbed to the top of a particularly high canyon (we were spoilt for choice with those), disconnected my gravity regulator and threw myself off. Big fall, big mess. End of story you'd think. But you'd be wrong. All of a sudden things got a whole lot stranger. I woke up back on Earth.

Or did I? I regained consciousness of sorts, buried in the wall of the bedroom I grew up in during my teenage years. Except that time had moved on. It was covered in dust and dishevelled boxes of old books and musty-smelling clothes in exactly the way my mother would never have allowed it to degenerate when I was at home. I moved, or tried to, and I sort of succeeded. A bit. I persevered. Gradually I detached myself with a sort of sticky swishing sound and floated across the room. I looked down. I hung in space from a viewpoint about seven feet above the floor. I seemed to have no body, but as I experimentally thrashed some limbs around I began to notice some minor distortions in my visual field. Gradually I began to perceive that I possessed a kind of ghost form, a near-transparent trace-image of my erstwhile naked living body. Now I don't do spooky supernatural. I'm using the term *ghost* here as a best-fit metaphor. I already had the basics of a theory forming in my head as to what I might be observing and experiencing. Remember I'm an astronaut. Panic is not in the behavioural lexicon. I seemed to be in no physical pain, so my scientific curiosity was soon taking me over. Slowly my fascination grew into something approaching exhilaration. I flew around the room, I buckled against the ceiling, I swept down to the floor, hid in corners. Then I tried to leave the room and hit a fundamental problem. I had no hands, or none sufficiently materialised. For a moment I felt trapped and scared and then my imagination saved me with a simple proposition: was my transparency more than visual, could I move through walls? The same method of concentration that enabled me to fly, it turned out, could be deployed to make me pass through solid surfaces. Turns out it gets easier after the first time, because you know what you're imagining and what you are asking yourself to do. So I did it. I can't say it feels very pleasant, but I passed through a door, then a wall. I would later find out that I could even get through lead and six-feet thick concrete, it just took a little more effort.

Once I was through that door, the world opened up before me, a panoply of possibilities. But with one disturbing drawback: an apparent inability to communicate. There was my aged mother in the kitchen, hobbling about in her furry slippers, struggling to remember how to boil a pot of potatoes, putting on her radio to hear if there was any news about her beloved son missing presumed dead on the distant planet of Yttria. I wished I could talk to her. I tried to shout out but I had no lungs, no vocal cords apparently. I even tried squeezing my way through her skull and into her brain eventually, in utter desperation, but it's all just white mush and electrical flashes in there, I can tell you authoritatively. I wanted to tell her what I knew, or what I thought I knew: that the duplication process had gone wrong, but saved my life in the process; that killing my duplicated body on Yttria had not killed me, but left my soul, my spirit, my whatever, in some kind of limbo, trying to find its way back inside its original body still strapped down on a bed in the Telepedrome in Nevada. Unless... now this was too horrible to think about. Unless that terrorist attack had destroyed my sleeping body at Nevada, and this spirit, this me, had nowhere left to go home to.

What a moment when we first set eyes on Yttria. Eyes first, then feet. The five duplication pods were rolling back, a light mist of humidity dispersing, and each of us was waking up, drowsy and stunned, on our first alien planet. Ellie had "arrived" a minute before us and had just finished sending the panoramic security shutter back up into the roof housings. Those glittering grey mountain ridges were like the back of a gargantuan iguana, towering into the sky. Yttria's skies were shades of orange and crimson by day, a wild set of greens at dawn and dusk: olive, emerald, mint and teal. Arturo Akamatsu just began laughing spontaneously at the sheer terrifying beauty of it, I remember that distinctly. Setting off Valerie Fornara into increasingly hysterical giggling, the first sign perhaps of the bond that would later form between them. They hugged shortly after they'd staggered to their feet, and as Ellie turned around at the window: the three of us, Ellie, Kurt and myself, all just stared quizzically at each other and slowly smirked, like kids with a big brand-new toy.

There wasn't much time to sit around and marvel of course. So many checks to be done, not least on our own physiology, that nothing had gone wrong in the quantum entanglement process. We could hear the rounds of applause only now subsiding over the ansiblecom from Nevada. How casually we accepted that technological marvel of instant umbilical connection back then, unaware of the horror of living without it that was to come. It took us the first two weeks to assemble our five personal aerial reconnaissance craft from the manageable kit sections ansibled out by NASA. Arturo was our biology specialist, Kurt our geologist, Valerie our climatologist and chemist, Ellie our physicist and astrophysicist. I was the linguist and psychologist, so had the least to work on (in terms of analysing soil and atmosphere samples) until we actually found alien life. The probespores had provided tantalising glimpses over the preceding few months; we believed we might find subterranean invertebrates, colonising the fertile margins around active volcanic vents. We'd seen large reddish worms fleetingly, from the probes, but everything had been inconclusive so far, distant and grainy and blurred with mist and steam and camera shake. We just had to get out there, boots on the ground, but the distances were vast, the terrain vertiginous and potentially unstable. We needed flight and fuel, utilising the atmospheric consistency and pressure for uplift, metabolising its constituents for controlled combustion. Not just us but the best brains on Earth were simultaneously working on it. They got there. Our gadgets arrived and we assembled and tested them. Sun-up on the fifteenth day, we donned our oxygen masks and gravity regulators and walked out of the airlock one by one, NASA's voices buzzing

like deranged bees in our ears, monitoring our
breathing and heart-rate with frenzied trepidation.
Again some of us found ourselves laughing
involuntarily. They made us feel like miracles,
supermen and superwomen. We were just living and
breathing after all, and not going crazy, not yet, and it
felt good.

Oh but where would I go now? Back on Earth I who
was now free to drift anywhere, with no body, ageless,
aimless. I was like some kind of dark silent fish,
swimming indolently through the dark reed-beds of
terrestrial life. I thought of my four duplinaut
companions as trees, mysterious new trans-stellar
trees, whose canopies sprouted and spread eighty-four
trillion miles away on Yttria, though their fantastically
distended trunks, their temporal pasts still sat deep-
rooted into Earth's brown soil. You see? My concept of
time and space has evolved to become somewhat
different from yours. So would yours in comparable
situations, after comparable experiences. Not that such
experiences are at all comparable to anything of
course. I got bored, and not a little sad, with watching
my aged mother potter about the house and
wondering what she was thinking and how to
communicate with her. In the end, I drifted out
through the walls and roof of that place, leaving my
childhood home behind, draped as it was in cobwebs
and melancholy memories. If I could pass through
walls and space at will, then why not time? Hovering
above the suburban driveway in the sharp spring light,
might I not conjure up the spectre of my youthful
father, pulling up there in the early 2270s in his dark
umber Wolseley Six, newspaper under his arm, soft
pork pie hat on his balding pate, a box of mint
meringues in his hands as a treat for his wife and kids

after a hard week at the office? My memories became very real to me in this strange disembodied state, with so little else to distract me.

I remember Ellie telling me about her childhood memories, one fine red Yttrian afternoon as we found ourselves walking together through a vast prairie of brown cauliflowers, as we nicknamed them, whose tall canopies flapped in the breeze six feet above us as we wove between their trunks like little black ants. The mysterious plants, which Arturo had been analysing samples of frantically since we first brought off-cuts back to him, now appeared to be about to blossom. Purple protuberances were emerging from the black skin, swelling into odd star-shapes, acquiring a turquoise blush at their tips.

Ellie said this reminded her of where she grew up in the mid-west, a little township of white timber houses in Iowa, surrounded by cornfields whose green stalks she and her brother used to run through on summer mornings. She said this with a gentleness, with an intimate tone of voice, that I had not heard her use before. That strange environment beneath the canopies gave our voices an odd acoustic resonance to start with, but I felt also, especially when she turned and looked at me, her blue piercing eyes rifling me for a reaction; that some unexpected new bond was forming between us. We had heard our first Yttrian language the week before, and she had been deeply fascinated by my initial techniques for deciphering it.

Shortly after that we came to an unexpected bluff, and stood together at its edge, gazing down into a transfixing sea of liquid mercury out of which strange yellow helicopter-flies were bubbling up like steam. A sudden sound made us jump, for a moment Ellie even involuntarily clinging to me in fright. We looked up: it was Kurt Arnott breaking the sound barrier by taking the freight loader home faster than NASA guidelines,

spangling green light of the first tinges of sunset
bouncing off its silver bodywork as it crossed the sky
in a couple of heartbeats. We spun around. The red
stamens on all the trunks of the brown cauliflower
trees were suddenly bursting open, spewing blue light
and twinkling sound across our field of view. Closing
our helmets over for extra caution, we made our way
back through the magical and perplexing display,
trying to catch a few of the blue lightflies, puzzling
over whether they were animal or plants or some
unfathomable hybrid of the two.

So back here on drab old Earth: shall I go now to
Iowa, to the white shiplap and the waving corn,
inspired by that recollection of Ellie's recounted
childhood? Fly through those more familiar terrestrial
green stalks on lazy summer days, lie back and gaze up
at the endless blue skies and white wisps of dreamy
cumulous? Or to San Francisco, where her family
moved to later, that city I will always associate with
winter lights and urbane wealth, the hedged gardens
of Pacific Heights and Russian Hill where she spent
her teenage years? Search there for any traces of her?
Bask in the sublime bittersweet residue of blighted
and unrequited love? Or explore my own life first?
Cross the highways and railways and fields and hills
until I reach that bleak eastern city from where my
estranged wife last wrote to me, telling me of the first
signs of her building a new life, starting a new
relationship with someone from her office? It was me
who left her after all, chose space and risk over staid
middle-aged security. I left as a man, albeit one with
an odd existential bent and immunity from
commonplace pleasures, but here I am returned as an
angel, a demon, who knows which. A spirit, a ghost
man, who can travel like electricity across the globe,
map the nodes of his body onto city grids, meld his
thoughts with the weaving pathways of buses and

tramcars, his breath become the sigh of the evening wind, his dreams the last glimmer of sunset light in a million attic windows glimpsed from the last train home.

The five of us got into our little silver hover-spheres and took to the crimson skies of Yttria, laughing like school children, singing over the intercoms, accompanied by a swarm of twenty silver probespores like a flock of geese or a pack of hunting dogs, who could sniff out all the nooks and crannies of the planet's insane topography quicker and more nimbly than we could. We still believed the planet was relatively barren then, were yet to see its many wonders mysteriously unfold.

Some strange barrage of clouds was forming off to the west above a vast grey desert plane, getting Valerie Fornara worried as she ran her meteorological predictions through a series of algorithms. Red dust, composed mostly of iron ore, but forty per cent Yttrium particles, deadly to human lungs. If a storm came in we would have to lie low to conserve oxygen and all but shut down our atmospheric filtration kits. That was the day we found The Great Fold, as we christened it, an elongated cave entrance twenty-six miles across, under and into which it was possible to fly down into a near-surface concealed depression approximately sixty miles in diameter. Hidden from the sky and the dust storms, hidden from above altogether, but teaming with life. Worm colonies we called them at first, although I would later come to recognise them as what they truly were: cities of an alien civilisation unimaginably different from our own.

I went there. I couldn't resist it. I clung to some lorries

on the interstate, then willed myself up to play pleasantly among the wings of migratory geese. Then I saw a Boeing 898 overhead and swooped up to cling onto the bodywork of that. I could rise and fall like water vapour, I found my moods changed with cloud formations. Eventually I fell down slowly, see-sawing like a fragment of burning paper from a bonfire, landing on the roof of the bungalow in suburban Boston which I'd once shared with my wife. I clung to the ceiling like a fly. I rolled across the endless landscape of patterned wallpaper as their talk droned on down below. I watched her and the new man flirt and ceremoniously and symbolically dance around each other in conversation, as is the tedious human way. I watched them make indifferent love afterwards as I clung to the ceiling with the detachment of an alien insect. It wasn't sad or sordid. It was shockingly invigorating to see everything that enchants and intimidates us during our lives in this world finally reduced to something meaningless and animalistic. I no longer had any gender, never mind sexual desires. I had become a god at last. But who to tell?

So many fires. Glowing lights in vast arrays below us. Inside their bodies, inside their strange architecture which they seemed to weave from the Yttrian mud and sand, mixing it with secretions from their lymph nodes. They appeared to have various antennae and grasshopper-like limbs on their upper bodies. This light from within was flashing on and off constantly, pulsing, modulating. I knew it must be communication, music or mathematics. They were like ants but more advanced. I immediately began recording as much of their chatter as I could. We could detect it in the infra-sound range, a kind of clicking and droning, but I suspected I would need to pair this with the visual data before setting the computers loose on it. We came back with the larger group reconnaissance vehicle, Kurt at the controls while I tried to livestream the data. I kept asking Kurt to turn around and go back for another loop and fly over their amazing cities. Lower, lower, I begged him.

Of course we took it too far in the end. On the third day, the Yttrians sent up some kind of primitive flying-machine to try and intercept us. It got too close, it was their own fault. Made of some kind of flimsy sail-like material braced with struts of a bamboo-type rigid stalks. Sort of like a fast balloon, but more manoeuvrable, powered with a burning gas mixture, probably mostly methane. It snagged in the intake of the reconnaissance freighter's magnetosphere, blew the craft and its occupant apart. We retrieved all the falling fragments and took them back to the base station for analysis, but I felt terrible at having killed one of those things on our very first contact. It didn't seem to bode well at all for the future of the interaction of our two species. Ellie and Valerie and Arturo shared my horror, tempered only with the excitement of the ongoing autopsy made possible by the organic remains now at the disposal of Arturo to dissect and X-ray. But Kurt, whose actions, although probably unavoidable, were more instrumental in the alien death than anything else, seemed oddly calm and reticent. Perhaps he was stunned or in denial, but his attitude irked me. I caught him singing quietly to himself in the base canteen as he warmed himself his milk drink at lights-out, suddenly stopping when he heard me enter the room. I knew we were all trained to be composed and ultra-calm, but was all this some kind of boy-scout day out to him? Had he no sense of the enormity of our responsibility?

I eventually decoded transmissions from within the Great Fold. The Yttrians had something akin to television. They were sharing reports of sightings of us, but the majority of Yttrians, including those in charge, didn't seem to believe a word of them, kept coming up with other explanations: that we were sunspots, ball lightning, interference, white noise, dead insects on their lenses. I wondered what we'd have to do to be real to them, why they found it so hard to believe in our existence.

On earth I decided a romantic visit to Ellie's childhood haunts could wait. I felt profoundly transformed by having watched my ex-wife with her legs in the air. A more practical theorem began to intrigue and then possess me. Kurt Arnott's past, as he had related it to me in various conversations: was it fact or fiction? It's surprising how hard you can concentrate when you don't have a physical body to distract you, how accurately you can move your mind back through time and recall all your memories of past conversations in detail. I went to his supposed neighbourhood in the Bronx, where he claimed to have grown up in impoverished circumstances. I looked for his address, the apartment on the corner overlooking Soundview Park. I found his parents, but they were nothing like he described. Retired police ostensibly, CIA actually. A picture emerged and rapidly began to change, became a very different one from what he had painted. The more I hung around there eavesdropping the more I began to feel something, faintly at first, a weird kind of drag being exerted, some kind of force from an unseen direction. It was like a kind of tractor-beam. NASA had detected me in the household of Kurt Arnott's parents and were drawing me towards Nevada somehow. It was a bit like sexual attraction at first, come to think of it. You know. The way you kid yourself on it's something else, something rational, something you really want to do for some noble non-physical reason. But before you know it you're flying up the highway towards bad-idea city with no brakes and no possibility of a safe off-ramp.

So Kurt Arnott was a fraud. A sleeper agent for dark forces, vested financial interests, right-wing militarism. I was drawn magnetically like a squirming blob of liquid metal, across the states and across Nevada, into the heart of the telepedrome, a concrete maze with a series of sixteen-feet thick solid lead doors closing behind me. I finally came to rest within some sort of prepared containment zone, a committee room with a round table of top brass military minds and scientific consultants all looking at me curiously. They had engineered an electromagnetic spectrometer, a new-fangled quantum filter to make me visible. Their Chairwoman, someone I had never seen before, a new Telepedrome Director, discussed me in hushed tones for five minutes with her advisors then turned towards me and addressed me like some crazed caged beast.

Oh my. What creeps, what devious conniving liars they had all been. There had been no terrorist attack on the Telepedrome, no need to sever the link with our mission after all. It had all been a sham, she admitted, part of some bizarre biological and strategic territorial experiment. They had needed us to start a colony. They had needed us to completely believe that our isolation was accidental, was total and irreversible. *Why?*—I raged, my voice now strongly audible with a kind of sinister metallic vibrato, amplified within the quantum cage.

Galactic law, Director Lila Selznick answered me, *as imposed by the Creflastrians. We can't colonise alien worlds except by fatal misadventure. Plausible deniability. In a hundred years, there will be a thousand humans there, then they'll be officially Yttrians, and the planet's resources will be ours to mine freely. Yttrium, a rare earth metal, a vital component in all our quantum processors, in all our nano-tech engineering. You wouldn't be standing there without it, Major Aslaug.*

I wish I wasn't standing here, I answered, *except that I'm not standing here. I have no legs, no anything anymore.*

Well now, Selznick smiled half-heartedly, *we can help you with that, if you cooperate. In some ways we wish you weren't standing there either. This wasn't supposed to happen. Your suicide, your self-indulgent, self-pitying personal psychological implosion was very human in retrospect, but damned inconvenient. You're a right royal pain-in-the-ass, make no mistake. But we're glad we've found you now, actually, truth be told. Things haven't been going entirely to plan on Yttria, while you've been away, you see, and what with time dilation and differential space-time distortion due to Yttria's much greater planetary mass than Earth's, that's rather a long time you've been away in their terms. You following me? It occurs to us that you could be the perfect answer, the perfect way for us to lend a secret hand to our supposedly hopelessly-abandoned and isolated de-facto colony-in-waiting on Yttria.*

What if I say no? I asked and waited for my chilling echo to dissipate around the chamber.

Selznick smiled like she'd long seen this one coming. *Major Aslaug, tell us, how does it feel to be dead? Just think of all that reflective wisdom you've been able to amass for these last few months of hanging around everybody's ceilings. Wouldn't you rather be born again?*

Born in Glasgow in 1967, **Douglas Thompson** *won the Herald/Grolsch Question of Style Award in 1989, 2nd prize in the Neil Gunn Writing Competition in 2007,* *and the Faith/Unbelief Poetry Prize in 2016. His short stories and poems have appeared in a wide range of magazines and anthologies, including Ambit, New Writing Scotland and Albedo One. His first book, Ultrameta, published by Eibonvale Press in August 2009, was followed by eight subsequent novels and short story collections: Sylvow (Eibonvale Press, 2010), Apoidea (The Exaggerated Press, 2011), Mechagnosis (Dog Horn Publishing, 2012), Entanglement (Elsewhen Press, 2012), The Rhymer (Elsewhen Press, 2014), The Brahan Seer (Acair Books, 2014), Volwys (Dog Horn Publishing, 2014), and The Sleep Corporation (The Exaggerated Press, 2015). A new combined collection of short stories and poems The Fallen West will be published by Snuggly Books in late 2017/early 2018. His first poetry collection Eternity's Windfall will be published by Red Squirrel in early 2018. A retrospective collection of his earlier poetry, Soured Utopias, will be published by Dog Horn in late 2018. Yttrium Part 1 is taken from his novel Barking Circus, forthcoming in 2018 from Eibonvale. Part Two of "Yttrium" will be published in TQF61.*

Amongst the Urlap

Andrew Peters

There is a poem, or rather a ditty (the Urlap holding poetry in low regard) that has been faithfully but unimaginatively translated to a *ruba'i* by Sursock, thus:

> *On the rising of my root I'll state my case,*
> *Our pact I'll seal with plunging of my mace.*
> *We'll haggle 'neath the bowl of seven moons,*
> *My word, my deed, as honest as my face.*

As with the entire oral tradition, the final word is repeated six times with a specific pattern of emphasis, in this case Quilliam and Price's P-URL4. To hear it is quite a thing. It comes at you from that vibrating abdomen in shocking waves, repulsive, compelling. The thrumming gaining force from the fact that above all that lower-body action the shells of those Urlap faces, darkly polished as chestnuts, remain impassive, cool as you like. It's a biological quirk, this limited facial range, nobody has suggested an evolutionary advantage to it. But it just so happens that their poker faces make them wonderful negotiators.

Note, please, the poem's sexual imagery. Much has been written on the conjunction of commerce and sex for the Urlap, anyone approaching this complex subject has hundreds of books and hollies to choose from. None of them, of course, fully prepare you for the first time you sit down to negotiate with one of them, or – as is more often the case – a nicely oiled row of them, and that chitinous phallus springs upwards from the sacrum.

Just keep looking at the eyes, we are taught, *ignore what's going on down there at the waistline*. For the Urlap, you see, find it uncivil not to demonstrate their pleasure in the transaction. Naturally, they think us coarse for not doing the same. There we sit, eyes locked, reminded of our differences, each of us busy forgiving the other.

It wasn't easy for Elizabeth. We sat close together, Urlap style, our shoulders touching, and when we got to the part of the deal exciting for our hosts, sitting opposite, and all that leathery unfurling began around their groins I felt her stiffen. She made a slow stricken clearing of the throat. A look of reassurance would have been appropriate here, a pat on the hand, but we were talking money at last, which was probably what had got the blood up in Prince Nank, and so I chattered on and felt her loosening beside me as she remembered her training.

This was in the Prince's flesh-coloured parlour. One of the finest rooms on the planet, with a low autumn sun pushing through the windows and painting us in a sort of tender firelight. Ochre, burnt umber, a level pour of vermillion along the horizon which turned the Prince's yellow carpet pink. If it wasn't for all that new weight wanding around the princeling's middle we would be having a civilised time of it in this room, partaking in an old-style reception. The setting, in fact, was something like the courtly style of Earth. While Nank chortled on through his translator I distracted myself with the Louis Quatorze chairs – Nank is a true Terraphile – and the prints of Aertsen's *Butcher's Stall* and the *Flight into Egypt* which enlivened one of the wainscoted walls. There was also a fine reproduction Babson globe sitting in tilted poise on his desk.

But at last I gave in to a downward glance and heard myself say: "I see we have gained your interest, Your Highness."

Overly forthright, probably. Certainly not in any training manual, such an obvious reference to the body. Elizabeth, newly qualified, later remonstrated with me. Foolishly, fatally, I replied that sometimes you have to step away from what you know. For now, though, all went brilliantly. The Prince, probably not expecting anything so candid, paused for a moment and then clicked into the translator something which came out as "Interest equates totality of zero" (those things never do well with epigrams) and went into a hissing chuckle that we warmly echoed.

Oh, we were all in a fine humour. The evening helped us on our way. The onset of an Urlap night is a thing of solemn richness, uplifting, what with all that browning upper light and below the late flare of the city's stone. The crimson disc drops quickly and the surrounding hills dissolve, you can count them going ("Seven hills for seven moons", is the old saying), and when all the turbulent stone has gone there are only the glinting lines and tubes of the city's commerce, silvered lattice, and the sombre giant glaring of the Urlap windows.

There I was, drunk on weather. I blurted out our first offer a week before we had intended to. Another rule broken. Old Nank should have kicked us out, but he is enough of an Earthling to ignore the clumsiness (he has a good Tantalus on his sideboard filled with nectary liquids which resemble, in hue at least, whiskey and brandy). The tightly strung football of head dipped towards the translator and he informed us with much formal clicking and clacking that we would meet again in a week's time.

Out we bowed, grinning, pressing our hands to our hearts. The walk back to our quarters was short, a matter of a few corridors. Was I surprised to see Elizabeth already slithery and floppy for Nank? There is not so much literature on this, but the phenomenon is well known. As soon as the Prince's door was closed on us she opened up in a sort of green-leafed joy about Nank's high bearing. He was a "class act". The Prince had been "so refined" about my early offer, even though he had every right to decline it then and there, he was so "gracious" about my slip was the sum of it.

"Bullshit," I said, "I know Nank's type and I know how quickly we can go with him. And I wouldn't grant him so much for the title if I were you, half the planet is a marquess or prince or grand duke. They've got so many of them they don't know what to do with them all. That's why old Nank spends his days buying antiques."

But she was full of him already. "Prince Nank is one of the most well connected princes on the planet." She sent the last word out on a cushion of exasperation. *PLAH-net.*

"Oh come on, they're *all* well connected. That's what being a prince is about. Ever heard of a prince with shitty connections? You put one out of shape and the whole lot of them come after you."

"Yes, but he's Prince *Nank*, you can't go anywhere here without hearing what Prince Nank has to say about something. He's everywhere, involved with everything."

So she had set him up on such high ground already. Naturally, with something so elevated, the thing to do is go scrabbling and clambering after it. Disappointed in her, I said nothing for a while.

We walked across the Nephra Bridge. The sun was just about gone, there was only some blue bruising over our heads and a sort of sludge of burgundy surrounding. Against the windows of the bridge there rolled the thin nectarine mist that sometimes comes up in the evenings.

Things were better back at our suite. Our quarters are a carefully worked out set of Earth angles on the upper floors of the Diplomatic Block. "Let's have some noodles," she said. Her hand came out and gave my waist a pinch. She laughed. "Don't you fancy some noodles?"

Our apartment, you see, is full of them. The Chinese were here six months ago and left the storage units and the spaces under the beds packed tight with the candy-coloured stacks. Oh, the ingenuity! I smiled bitterly at Commander Wang's joke as I searched them for bugs, compelled to open countless packs at random to check the contents. The waste disposal unit was soon full of them, piled like the tiny white bones of shrews or voles. The presence of these things in the sink units, the wall storage, even within the spaces of the entertainment console, rubs at Elizabeth's high tilt of humour. Wang's cleverness has become one of her small joys, just as potent to her as the steel blue sunrise which she stretches to each morning at the panoramic window and the howl of the wind around the building when a mesospheric storm dips down to touch the Tangn Plain.

In search of goodwill we timed our arrival for the hundredth anniversary of First Contact. The day after touchdown we were led to the Grand Assembly for the ceremony. Short enough, a speech and a recitation of the Urlapian Creed performed as a fugue beginning at one end of that dank chamber and circulating along the ribs of obsidian thrones until the drone reached the necessary pitch. We stood in the wet air, a night sea with the whalefall of the fossilised Father at the centre of the floor guarded by four attendants in rich heraldry (the helms and crests etched directly onto the plates of the skin). Our allotted place was near the entrance, where the ammoniac stench of so much Urlapian breath was softened by the air admitted from the Hero's Gallery. From here we could be easily presented to the surviving member of the first crew, the Marquess (*Crrrt*, one rank beneath *Crrrc*, or Sovereign Prince) of New Delhi, who is therefore also the only living Urlapian to take a terrestrial designation.

The Marquess is held up by the Urlap as an Armstrong or a Vela, as a sort of king of space whose long and burnished face stares down from a million walls. His public appearances are rare. It is rumoured that the King, jealous of his stature, restricts him to only a few a year, and therefore when he comes amongst the people there is spontaneous and sonorous joy. And so it was this time. The hooting went up and I turned to see the knot of his entourage push through the great doors, and at the head of it Sir Kann, the chief of protocol, scampering sideways as he attempted to direct the lot of them towards us. His clacking drowned out by the giant drone that was just finding the sweet edge of delight and welcome, Sir Kann at last got the group to turn in our direction. Presently the huddle paused and parted so that the Marquess could be presented.

Divine the thoughts of an Urlap, whether the pebble of eye holds mirth, grief, love or hate? The task is beyond us. We cannot even guess their age. Their facial plates do not with advancing years fall into slings and swags like our poor covering, lacking ectodermal tissue. Although the face is not, as nearly every schoolchild today incorrectly supposes, part of an exoskeleton.

By the time we are about to topple into the grave, your Urlap is merely browning a little along the raised seams of the skin, as brass carelessly polished. All the tautness of the jaw and cheekbones remains. There is no retreat of the eye or slackening of the mouth, their hairless skulls are not marbled by the sun. They slow a little, perhaps. But even then there is none of the submissive bending and curling of the human, so that an Urlap goes to his deathpit undiminished, the straightness of youth residing to the end, which is usually well into the second century.

And so the Marquess who stood before us was little changed from the co-pilot who stood once on Indian soil, in the dying light of the White Salt Desert of Kutch, to listen to his captain reply to President Singh's welcome speech ("We who heard the beating of another's heart across the void have come in peace to join it... *et cetera*). He looked us over. They are instructed to ignore our jelly torsos in the same way that we are taught to overlook their priapism, but they can't help but scan us all the same. Then we got his formal clicks, a long burst, as he extended his hand. A rare thing, the Urlap handshake. Most won't do it even should you forget yourself and hold out your own. Only the higher orders and the few that have travelled to us will gladly offer it.

The hand came to me first and I shook it and, returning the favour, gave an Urlapian shimmy of the head. He turned to Elizabeth. She grabbed his hand, pumped that brittle palm, started upon a speech, parataxical, platitudinous ("An honour... so much time... always dreamt of this moment... such bravery") which cut across all Urlapian etiquette and had the Marquess nodding in confusion and Sir Kann scrambling for a translator before I could stop him.

Now, the Marquess looked his century and more. He sank an inch as we stood there and listened to Elizabeth's dwindling flow ("...Wow... What a... what a... I mean, wow...") until, after much chirring, a translator was passed to the front and held under her chin. She had to start from the beginning – it was not clear if the Marquess could hear the translated splinters of sound – and she soon wound down to a mindless nodding and grinning. The Marquess took it well, the old head tilting this way and that on its mount, and made a reply that was rendered as "sinks the sink, nicely!" before being led away by Kann to the howl of the stadium.

"Why?" I asked her an hour later, as we made our way back to our quarters, our ears ringing, "Why did you decide to give the Marquess that little number? Poor Kann, he was too polite to shut you up."

She shrugged and blew a strand of damp hair from her face. "Fucking Kann, that's his job isn't it? He just *completely* pisses me off with all that bowing and scraping."

Kann who had spent a week before our arrival stocking our pantry and personally supervising the hunts for the meat served to us each evening. Kann, who had been the first to greet us on the landing ramp where, having forsaken our exercises, we stood with shaking knees and the vertigo of the newly stationary. Kann, who had left on our Egyptian cotton pillows poems of welcome printed in Gothic script on traditional Urlap paper (a variety of fibrous mould), endearingly misspelled.

"Fuck Kann, he drives me nuts," she finished with, and we went the rest of the way to our quarters in silence.

She can cut as a saw like this, when her mood turns. I saw it first mid-voyage when, browsing *Cosmo* or one of the other mags with which she filled the idle hours, she let out a bitter groan and hurled her water bottle across the cabin. Pushing off to float over her shoulder I saw an image of Otto Trott emerging from a nightclub with his arm slung low around the waist of a skinny girl under a giant poodle wig. I recognised her as a minor holli personality and half-remembered the chorus of the song that had made her name.

"That fucking *bitch*, look at her!" She slumped under the affront, rose again to peer more closely at the screen. "They're practically riding, the way she's jamming her butt into him. I can't believe he'd do a thing like that, I mean what's he playing at?"

"I didn't know you were a fan of Otto Trott," I said.

"I used to date him."

"You dated him? *The* Otto Trott? The musician?"

She had a picture of him on her V which she showed me with a nervous hand. There he lay, black muscle squeezed from white shorts, disinterestedly regarding the lens as the bed sheets roiled round him, one arm thrown behind the head to show a rich spray of hair, the other arm ending with the pearlescent nails scratching the drum of belly.

That is our Elizabeth Cowper-Delaney. All kinds of high Earthly connections. She has aristocratic legs, powerful in the thigh for horse-gripping, thick aristo hair also, doublehair, highly polished. Square features, very fine really, small around the nose, closely sanded all over. Probably why she was chosen to deal with the caste-bound Urlap. But now furious right down to the gizzard, all kinds of base squirtings taking place in the vital glands, primeval sludges sluicing around her thought centres. Reduced for the moment to jealous mate. Otto Trott's crime, she expressed through many hard words, rough statements, was everlasting, the wound eternal. It took her the whole evening to recompose herself, during which time I drifted in giant, remote exile near the forward porthole, through which the disc of Urlap could already be discerned.

The meat (*Fal*, a synonym for inedible) they bring us is

in taste and texture somewhere between pork and chicken. It is served each evening under a pewter cloche by the waiter we have dubbed Runcible, who looks after us for two forty-hour lunar days at a time. Runcible the Second takes over for a further half-day to complete what you might call the Urlapian week. The Urlap, of course, do not eat meat. The closest they come to it is during the feast days on which they consume large quantities of the *Snnk*, fish-like in biology, that you can see whitely suspended in their subterranean hatching pools, silent as a thought in a dark mind. The *Snnk*, insensible, unmoving, are easily harvested in nets and are eaten with *Satha*, a sort of honey derived from the excrescences of the irascible *Caff*, and so congealed that it is almost unworkable by the human jaw.

It was thoughtful of the Urlap to provide us with this meat which they find so repulsive. They hunt it especially for us on the Tangn, and it is afterward skinned and cooked by unfortunate chefs. Whenever one of the Runcibles lifted the cloche to release an impatient billow of steam and reveal the sweating slices we made sure to *umm* and *ahh* appreciatively, which was always answered with a happy chirr and a shallow bow.

Until the change in arrangements we sat, whenever we were both at home for the evening, at either end of a walnut dining table separated by a candelabrum. Certain that the room was monitored, we discussed any of a range of banal topics: the possibility of another storm, the tenderness of the *Fal* or *Snnk*, the merit of a new trade agreement of which we might have read on the Nooz, the capital adequacy of the Ethiopian banking sector, any old thing to occupy their analysts. Sometimes, operating expertly from within the liquid ripple of her cocktail dress, Elizabeth would convey to me her efforts to evade Nank's advances, which she half-pretended to deplore. All in a sort of code, naturally.

"I feel a headache coming on," she might start with, settling her knife and fork on her plate. "Such a pity as I have a date with the Prince tonight." An impish glance in the candlelight. We could both see the voyeuristic Nank in his distant apartments clenching his fists and tearing out his earpiece.

Sometimes she would be the Southern Belle, wriggling her shoulders and rising in her chair: "I do dec-*layah*, but there wasn't but a little pushin' and shovin' at the ball last night. It was all ah could do to keep my stays from burstin', the place was so hog-wild." Oh yes, poor Nank, you had to conceive it, confronted with the garbled translation in the dark well of his bedpit.

On rare occasions she would carry this act into the lounge or kitchen, and with a tormenting grandiloquence of human gesture perform for the hidden cameras and microphones grotesque scenes of suffering passion: "Oh my damn my guts," couch-prone, one arm thrown over the brow, the other tearing at the bloused belly while the legs thrust and pumped frog-like, "my damn *guts* are going to be the death of me, it feels like the bloody things are going to squitter right out."

What could Nank return from that, with his anchored eyebrows and bi-directional lips? His range was too close, Urlappian, no match for her. Yes, if we could know the code of his shivering pupils (Frater and Eiesenstadt have started here, at least, but only just) we might see an answer, but for now the truth of him, whatever it is, remains behind the baffle of his difference.

Once, after we had sat in silence for a couple of evening hours in the marsh-light of our V screens, she rolled towards me in her chair and, in a tone of distilled seriousness and yet with a diacritical arching of an eyebrow (a certain sign of jest) asked if I thought it might be possible to fall pregnant to an Urlap.

I thought for a while. In the corner of the window frame the bug disguised as an innocent screw waited. I fancied I could hear above me the whirr of the micro-lenses' micro-motors.

"Well," I began in mock thoughtfulness, "it has never been accomplished, at least as far as we know. But on Earth we have the example of the mule, and the goat-sheep, whatever it is called."

"The geep."

"Yes, the geep. And also the zorse and the grolar bear."

"Oh, yes, yes, yes," wriggling onto her front, a finger from extended arm pointing to the thought, "and the liger and the yakalo! There was a place back home that used to do yakalo meat. It was the most fabulous tenderest stuff."

"Yes, the yakalo and the wholphin. The wonderful wholphin. If we are to accept that sometimes nature rubs away our edges, then I suppose, in theory, with the Urlap we could make a variety of para-human."

She frowned and flipped onto her back, and didn't say anything for a while. We watched, instead, the distant launch of a Tranship. It slowly pulled its plume up the full height of the window before she answered.

"I don't think I should like that at all." She shook her head and fell silent for a minute, before she went on: "And I'm sure it would be beneath the Prince to father a Hurlap."

Somehow she had hidden this Urlap-love from the company. The company understands the power of a beautiful human in a certain stratum of Urlapian society, but there have been enough scandals and unpleasant incidents – Henny McCall-Clancy and Amelia Klumm-Edwards are only the most notable participants in a century-long string of amorous mishaps – for the company to include a "no contact" clause in the standard conditions of employment and introduce a ban on female-only trips (one which it will never publicly acknowledge, of course). And so they are plucked and filtered, sent aloft with a male of neutral attraction who the company can trust not to fall into bed with the hermaphrodite Urlap, and under threat of financial penalty they are asked to undertake the business with their legs clamped shut.

But it is an unfair requirement, once it's accepted that the Urlap are attractive to them. As soon as our Earth ladies land they are a rare prize, pursued by even the lowest ranks, rushed at with all manner of gift and warm offer – no wonder so many of them plunge. And she was aware of the speed of her own tumble.

"I won't be in for dinner, tonight," she said to me one evening, standing behind a fall of towel which she clutched under her chin in such a way as to leave a crescent of naked hip on either side of it. She had heard me returning from my weekly transmit and had come straight from the bathroom, leaving a silvered trail of shrinking footprints on the grey tiles.

"Oh?" I said, knowing already the meaning of the shifted glance, the manner in which one leg flexed impatiently to palpate the white cotton.

"Yes. I'm going to head out to dinner with Riikz. He called while you were out and I could hardly say no."

"Baron Riikz?"

"Yes, the Baron. He's such a nice guy, he really is." It was all there to see in the empty grin: violence, greed, shame, lust, she was coated and shining with it under the living-room spots.

"Now, you know what the..."

"Yes, I know, I know, I know. But Riikz is one of the

good guys, and he's very close to Nank, they're related somehow, some sort of cousins, I'm pretty sure of that." Her eyes looped as she considered the couplings in the copulation pits, the emissions and hot dabbings and deep absorptions and the quick slippery litters, jowl-to-jowl in the pod, which joined the prince and baron. "What we one-hundred-per cent *don't* want to do is piss off Riikz and blow the whole thing," she said.

"It would not be considered an offence if you simply told him..."

"But it's too late now. He caught me on the hop and I went and said yes, and now there's no way out of it. I mean, I can hardly V him and say I've changed my mind. That would be so rude."

"You can make an excuse."

"He would see right through it."

"So what? He'd think you were doing the proper thing."

"It would be an affront, it would be an insult."

"And what of it?"

"He could lean on Nank and get us thrown off the planet."

"That wouldn't be so bad. You know the company would rather we got deported than cause a scandal."

"Oh, don't be ridiculous. Scandal! I'm meeting Riikz for dinner, that's all. I'm not going to marry the guy." The grin had melted. My hysteria, as she later put it, ran straight through her, and she shook it out and thrust her hand through her wet hair and shook that out too with a dog's shiver so that the towel shifted to show the tender pink crinkling over her hip bone where her underwear had pinched her.

"You can wait up for me, if you like," she spoke as she turned for her room, not bothering to hide the steam-smarted rear, "to make sure he doesn't try to kiss me on the doorstep."

Riikz lasted a week or so. A couple of dinners and a

jaunt over the Zelln escarpment in his new Volanz, and with no contact at all by her account, no rubbing or tonguing or even a probing of his nether-jelly. I ascertained all this over a series of breakfasts during which she hung puffy-eyed above her bowl of reconchoc and shrugged away my questions with gruffly inflected grunts and groans. But I believed her. She is clever enough to know that her value to an Urlap, whose pride is as tender as a peach, lies in her mint condition, unsullied by a rival.

And so she climbed slowly and carefully through the court. After Riikz came Zafr, another baron but from a family closer to the Queen (if we are to believe there is a queen, after all), and then Viscount Bril, who rumour has it took a Chinese woman as consort for a while some years ago, before the Chinese made it their policy to send male-only crews.

Bril didn't want to let her go when the time came. He arrived at the door of our quarters one evening full of desperate twitching and demanded that I rouse her. It was well after midnight, and he could only be persuaded to leave by my describing, bent close to the translator so that I could whisper into the thing, the repulsive illness she was suffering, the sweats and puckerings and sulphurous blasts, every orifice in swollen flood.

"It is a human thing," I hissed as he creaked and champed above me, "it happens sometimes to us all."

The earls next, Fust and Rinq. Poor Fust was an easy victory. At a hundred and twenty he was old enough to have been considered for the First Contact flight, but had been looked over in the event. Perhaps his thirst for the human touch was derived from this ancient denial. He was certainly the most attentive of her beaux, arriving at the door exactly five minutes before each assignation and never complaining about being kept waiting a further fifteen, and sending all manner of gifts to our quarters at seemingly random intervals – a statuette of the Father wrapped in Urlapian green paper one cloudy lunchtime, and a day later the commemorative First Contact bowl which she began to use for her coffee each morning. Fust, she told me gleefully, wept when she informed him that her heart had warmed to another.

"Urlaps don't cry," I reminded her. We were in the gym room that had been kitted out by the Americans a half-century before, where the whir of the static bikes gave us a cover from the listening devices.

"I swear he did." Panting, her strong legs pumping the pedals, she pulled the end of the towel which hung around her neck across her face.

"They don't cry because they don't have tear ducts. There is no socio-biological mechanism that we would call crying. Bursting into tears for them is as impossible and meaningless as blowing bubbles of mucus from our ears would be to us."

"Blah, blah, blah. Why are you so hard on the Urlap?"

"I'm not being hard on them. It's just a fact that they don't cry, that's all."

"Well, Earl Fust did, when I told him last night that I wouldn't be able to see him any more."

"Impossible. You must have misinterpreted some other reaction."

"I'm telling you, he blubbed. He took a big gulp of breath," she took a gulp herself, "and his bottom lip began to vibrate and then he started to cry. It was so embarrassing for the poor guy. He sort of hid his face in his hands and I backed out of there as quick as I could."

"Impossible. He might have been having a breathless episode, the older ones get those all the time."

"Look, water came out of his fucking eyes. If that's not crying, I don't know what is."

"Some sort of condensation on the eyeball. Or a variety of eye disease, perhaps. There's so much we don't know about their pathologies." How could she know the shraums of an alien ailment?

"Jesus, the problem with you is that you just don't see how similar we are. Us and them. Human and Urlap."

"One can appreciate the differences and still see the similarities."

"I'm going to make one of them cry for you. I'll bring one of them back here and you can hide in the kitchen or something and jump out with your Scanz when I get the waterworks going. You could probably take samples and everything."

And she would have done this, I think, had not her next interest, Earl Rinq, been the proud Urlap he was. A scion of one of the military tribes, I had noted his overdeveloped limbs and outsize head at a number of social occasions. Poor old Fust, a distant relative, had invited him to meet Elizabeth at one of his evening soirees, and Rinq had simply announced at the end of the night that he would take her for himself. That's the gist of it, at least. The niceties were observed, no doubt, there would have been some courtly nodding and clacking in the corner of the room, but Fust would have foreseen his humiliation in the copulation pit had he refused.

"Did Rinq seek your permission, by the way, or did he just sling you over his shoulder?"

We sat in the lounge now, slippery bright from our showers. She sprawled in an easy chair and sipped her vitavit, her wet hair richly fallen on the towelling of her robe. The business of the early afternoon came to us distantly through the storm windows, engine whine and drill blast and slow-hooting traffic sirens made tiny by the glass.

"Oh dah-link," she threw her head back and patted the air with her hand, a Russian émigré for a moment, a White Russian princess playing an Istanbul piano for her supper with the sound of Red rifles in her ears, "he vas quite gracious about it. He said he vants me to try sahm of his spezial *Snnk* for ze vestival next week."

"The festival of what?"

Shrug. Frown. "The festival of whatever, how do I know? They have so many of them. He said he has the finest *Snnk* imaginable."

"And you said yes?"

"I said, 'what about Earl Fust? I'm sure he will invite me to have Snnk with him.' And he said not to worry about Fust, that he had squared it all off, but that I should inform him that I would not be in a position to sit with him again."

"Sit with him?"

"That's the way he put it. And Fust, of course, was watching us speak from the other side of the room, fiddling with his translator to see if he could catch any of our conversation, I suppose. I waited until he'd said goodbye to the last guest, I even stood next to him at the door like the good wifey as he hissed them off, and then I broke it to him. And that's when he cried."

She challenged me with a look. Fiercely it came to me over the rim of her glass. And so I decided to assert nothing more about the biology of the Urlap, and instead settled back in my chair to listen to Runcible's preparations for our supper, and his satisfied hum, halfway between a buzz and a purr, as he brought out the pots and unwrapped the meat.

The meat has become a problem. Our *Fal* began to run out a couple of weeks ago. The season is over, explained Sir Kann, strumming his chest with embarrassment. "The meadows are empty of the elders," he explained, "and the children must be forgiven, or the elders will be finished forever."

This, I assured him, is a problem with some species back on Earth. Nevertheless, he rumbled and sawed about it for a another quarter of an hour as Elizabeth walked in and out of the lounge preparing for her first date with Prince Nank. Kann must have known about Nank's battle with Rinq over the right to squire her, but he was good enough to avoid the subject completely, only glancing nervously towards her whenever he heard the approaching strike of her heels. She ignored him throughout, other than giving him a silent nod when he first entered.

I was glad to have Kann there, having feared ostracism after the scandal. Rinq had not gone so easily as old Fust. Their struggle had ended in the Council of Elders (from which grieving Fust excused himself as an interested party), where both of them had received a reprimand for their foolishness and been told that it was time for them to take good Urlap partners. I was informed by Kann that it had come very close to a duel, a phenomenon which no-one has seen for a hundred years or more, when a Viscount was decapitated and thereafter immortalised in "verse".

Nank's pitching himself at Elizabeth was no surprise. Our meetings grew increasingly convivial as we drew closer to a deal, and Elizabeth spent much of them engaged in wriggling flattery, her legs always bare and finely polished and never still as she bobbed and writhed in her seat at his attentions. We sat in his parlour and he would send all his anecdotes to her, I would get the occasional nod and chirrup only. He became showy in his Earthness, even attempting to amuse her with a human joke he had learnt ("an adult male walked into a restaurant with a winged animal on his shoulder...''). In return she gave him the pink volume of her laughing mouth, back as far as the epiglottis by the look of it, all the wet crimson promise of it she flashed at him as he looked on in delight.

I tried to warn her. "Look," I said, "hasn't this gone on for long enough, your fooling about with the Urlap?"

It was an early morning. She arched in the glow of her yoga mat, her pelvis pressed to the floor while her upper torso made a mermaid thrust for the ceiling and its painted sky. Her eyes remained closed as she responded levelly, without interest, "What do you mean, fooling about?"

The windows beyond her were filled with quicksilver dawn, a silken coiling of cloud was moved by the approaching sun. I stood by the breakfast bar, keeping a good distance, and spoke from behind my coffee mug.

"Well, I'm hardly counting, but how many has it been now?"

She exhaled through whitening nostrils. "And what does *that* mean? *Been*? Nothing has *been* in the way that you make it sound. Been! I've just dated a few, that's all."

"I'm not enquiring as to whether you've... I'm not interested in any of that."

"Yes you are. Of course you are, and don't think I don't know it. And the answer is no, I haven't. I'm not as stupid as you think I am, clearly." She flattened herself and rolled onto her back. The mat pulsed into dappled purple and the drawbridge of her legs went to the perpendicular. "I have dined with them, been entertained by them. And I'll probably get our deal closed in a single evening now that I'm seeing Nank."

"That's not the way we're supposed to do deals, you know that."

"There you go again. Insinuator."

"Not so. Revealear of truth."

"Oh, sure. Peddlar of prejudice. Hoarder of misconception."

"I'm worried, that's all. What happens when it all falls through with Nank? And don't say it won't, it's fallen through with the rest of them."

"Nank is different, he knows how we think. He is, in fact, the most Earthly Urlap I've ever met."

"Come on, you know better than that. Nank's no better or worse than the rest of them."

"How would you know? You don't know them at all."

"I know a few things about them."

"Really?"

"For instance, I know that their interest in the human female stems from her willingness to do things outside the copulation pits. They don't do that with each other, you must know that too."

She lowered her legs and remained still on the floor, eyes sealed. I continued: "Your realise that in their culture a private assignation is impossible outside marriage, the intimacy of it is intoxicating for them in a way that we could never comprehend. Just being on your own in a room with an Urlap is equivalent to..."

I was silenced by her scream. She flipped into a crouch and slapped the floor with her palms. "*Will* you just shut it? *Will* you just get over yourself?"

True heat in that stare, absolute human passion, the ragged unstable fringe of it. I moved quickly behind the breakfast bar and pretended to search for something. "I'm as worried for you as I am about the deal, if you really want to know," I said, scanning the counter for a teaspoon or bottle-opener, rattling a cutlery drawer open and shut.

"Don't be." She sprang upright and stalked off, whipping a towel over her shoulder. "Really. Don't be. Just don't ever talk about them like that again."

She slammed the door to the hallway behind her,

and in the repro-oak of one of the lower panels I saw the ghost of the repair where Rinq, unfamiliar with our door handles, had smashed his foot through it in pursuit of her.

That happened on the night on which she had called him to explain that she would not be free to join him for dinner, as Prince Nank had invited her to view one of his new mines. I had lain on the floor, batted there with an Urlap force which I had never imagined, and fumbled with my V to call Nank – having an idea that he could dispatch his palace guard to save us. But it was Rinq's own guard that ended it after all, rushing in from the corridor when they heard her screams and wrestling their master out of her room while I, on the floor, listened to the garbled nonsense from the translator which he had smacked from my hand: "For his Mudras food, stand by your hand, stand by your hand!"

She grew clever in our disputes. She liked to exalt the Urlap by first denigrating them, drawing me in. She did the same for Otto Trott, who she had not forgiven.

"I think he has an ugly face, don't you?" for example.

"Who?" I replied, pretending not to see the pic she fingered on her V.

"Otto. Look at him. Such a brute. His forehead is too big. Far, far, too heavy. You can hardly see his eyes under it."

"That's not very fair. He's concentrating on blowing into that thing. It makes it look like he's scowling."

"His eyes are half buried even when he isn't playing. Sometimes, if we were in a badly lit restaurant, I felt like I was sitting opposite a statue. You just can't see anything of the eyes at all, he's like one of those Easter Island heads."

"That must be disconcerting."

"You know, it could be frightening. It made me nervous if I couldn't see how he was looking at me."

"Eyes and souls, and all that."

"Exactly."

She shuddered, at the remembrance of him perhaps, and I too saw the dark cliff of him toppling over the napery. There was a pause, now that the value was established, this is how she slyly worked it. Then the curse was transformed: "But I suppose that's what gives him his power. I mean, when he's up on stage and lit by a spotlight, just a brilliant white light straight down from the gods, he *is* a thing of beauty, isn't he? Yes, he is, I think, rather irresistible at times like that. And I can't forget that the next time I see him, in a club or bar or back in his house, that's what makes me keep wanting to... oh," pinching the end of the canted nose, "s'cuse my bloomin' French, hahahahahaha." Turning serious, then: "But you know what I mean, don't you?"

Seriously, she stared at me.

That's how she proofed me against Otto Trott, and when she did the same with Prince Nank I hardly resisted. We were standing in the Chapel of Remembrance, where the human dead of a hundred years are entombed behind an obsidian wall, twelve plaques in three rows marking their places. 黄 and 鄭 and 范 are there. 林 of course, and 陳, who shares a row with Lambert, Widdicombe, and Mayer, and above them the Indians, Chandiramani, Padmasola, Kulkarni and Subramaniam. Three accidents on launch, two diseases (the Americans had wandered from their quarters in the days before effective inoculation) and a single suicide.

The Urlap have gone to great length to make everything correct. Giant candles stand in every corner, cross, crescent, hexagram and aum carved into the smooth wax. Above, a recessed light of carmine glass gives a soft darkroom glow. A pair of tapestries hangs opposite each other on the sidewalls: rainbows, winged cherubs, a squatting ganesha, star and crescent (crescent swallowing star), backdrop of alternately fecund and desert hills topped with stone keeps, fashionably lopsided, blank azure sky cornered with sun and moon, respectively. Simple wooden chairs line three sides of the room, a row of lumpen broken-backed hassocks runs beneath the wall of vaults. The floor is planked with rough imitation wood which gives a monkish sad-hewn feel to the place. The thoughtful roughness is only broken by a slender lectern in the corner, and the Urlap, of course, who on that storm-wracked evening – a terrible old blower had pushed down onto the Tangn and brought havoc to the plain dwellers – sat shining in the candlelight on two sides of the room while Elizabeth and I, honoured guests, had the back wall seats to ourselves.

Nank spoke at some length of the exploits of heroes and their eternal place in the heart (so said the translator) of the universe that is beyond all boundaries, both within us and without, and so on, all quite eloquently put and preprogged to avoid syntactical lunacy, and delivered in a stolid even cadence that we each somehow interpreted correctly to nod and sigh in the right places. I was invited to the lectern next and expressed our gratitude at their honouring of our dead, and gave a few lines of McCluskey – *to wonder at horizon-tooth of sail / and on the breath of dawn / pull oar towards it*, and so on – and then sat again for the Urlap to perform a lengthy grieving drone before leaving us alone to our own contemplations.

We stood for a while and listened to the tiny ripping of the air by the candles. From the corridor came the soft clicks of the departing Uralp, the cinching of the corridor air door. Then a deeper quiet.

Sombrely we stood and rocked on our heels, observing the black wall before us, neither of us wishing to break the silence. I thought of the men attached to the plaques, the names shining before us in deep-scored letters of gold, and wondered if any of the cadavers were really in the crypts – it is widely assumed that the Urlap would have taken the opportunity to dissect and experiment on those that had not been torched in rocket fuel – and if they were, how would they have fared in this strange Urlap air? I have seen corpses do quite well in the depths of Romanian monasteries and Egyptian caves. Sometimes the flesh persists, the stretched sheets of it around the prodding joints, weary brittle-sheeted carbon, you could blow all that away with a sigh. Macabre thoughts, certainly, but they allowed passage past darker possibilities.

"They really are a selfish species, in many respects." She seemed to jerk herself awake as she spoke, flipping into one of the side chairs.

"Who?" I said, checking behind us to make sure we were alone.

"The Urlap, of course. They are incredibly acquisitive."

"I suppose they are."

"Take Nank, for example, and all his antiques. You know, he can't stop talking about whatever is next on his shopping list. He's managed to get the schematics for a Han Dynasty burial suit from the New China Museum and is going to have it made here on Urlap, only in his size."

"The Prince has such good taste."

"It's a ridiculous outfit. There is a humungous codpiece stuck on to the front of it, which is a very Urlapian thing, don't you think? Do you think that's why he went for it?"

"Genitalia are central for them."

"This suit is all he can think of at the moment. He keeps dragging out the plans and showing them to me, and describing in *very* tedious detail the processes involved in making a jade substitute."

"He is something of a perfectionist, our Nank." I took a seat beside her and stretched out a little. It was good to sit there like that, in the warm quiet light of the chapel with its smell of wood and dust and hot wax.

"And before that it was a card table from the Met, even though he doesn't know the rules of a single card game, and next week I'm sure it will be something else. I know he's got his eye on some Crusader sword."

"Well, as you say, they are acquisitive."

"Incredibly so. And competitive. Nank nearly exploded the other day when he heard that Fann – you know the old councillor? – when he heard that he had got himself a replica pair of Napoleon's boots, made out of *Fal* leather. The real Napoleon, I mean, not the singer."

"What's the point of that? He'll never fit into them."

"That's what I said. *Look Nank*, I said, *how is an Urlap going to get into those things, anyway? And if you like them so much, why don't you just get a pair made for yourself the same way Fann did*?" She retracted her chin and flattened her mouth, gummily mummed Nank: "You cannot appreciate just how difficult it is to obtain *Fal* leather, my dear, the supply is finite."

"That's probably true. Kann said as much a couple of weeks ago, remember? Off-season, or something."

"Maybe. But it's the obsession that is so irritating. The way they let it drive them. It's unhealthy, if you ask me."

We sat for a while in silence, and I contemplated the dumpling sag of the hassocks and wondered what knees had left such impressions. We had knelt, that day, amidst the shades of all the great ones; the pioneers, statesmen, men of science and thought, poets even, Earth men who had made the swing across the void and paid their dues in this small chapel, before these quiet crypts.

"But I guess," she said, flicking an incisor with her finger (a habit with her), "that's the appeal of them."

"What is?"

"That they want us so much."

"You mean, like a collectible."

She flicked that away. "No, no. But it's the same drive, don't you see? To possess something completely. To own it all."

"This is desirable?"

"Yes."

"To be owned?"

"To be so wanted."

"Oh, to be *wanted*."

"Yes."

"And you are convinced that Nank wants you. I mean, not just as a... passing thing?"

She laid her hand on my forearm, but spoke to the opposite wall. "Yes. Yes, I am. He's asked me to marry him. He got down on one knee, Earth style, and said he would make me his wife."

Oh, unhappy Earth. Disconsolate parents. I spoke to Mr Cowper-Delaney myself, which she allowed as she refused to accept his incoming Vs herself, and the sad red bulbs of his eyes filled my screen, his wife invisible beside him but her sobs perfectly audible. Light years do not diminish misery and shock. These helpless parents pleaded for me to intercede.

I made a number of attempts to stop her, the last one on the night before the wedding when I came back from Kann's office. It had fallen to me to arrange the details of the ceremony with him. I entered our quarters to find her standing in the darkened living room, looking out at the biggest electrical storm we had seen that year. She clutched a glass of our precious rum to her chest.

"Well?" she said, when I was next to her.

"Kann has all the details fixed. The ceremony will be as Nank described it, more or less."

"More or less?" She was rubbery with drink and sleeping pills.

"There will be no Howl of Communion, or something like that. I mean, there's some protocol or other that..."

"I don't care about protocol. Will the wedding go ahead? Properly, I mean? Marriage?"

"Full Urlapian marriage. Nank will never set foot in a copulation pit again. Until the divorce, that is."

The edges of her mouth fell ragged, an elbow began to rise.

"Joke," I said.

"Joke, huh. You're so fucking funny."

The bellies of the far off clouds boomed electric blue and white, scattering veins of static across the Tolpn Hills. We waited for the sound to break against the storm windows, and when it did it splashed its capillaries of charge around the edges of the glass.

"Like Christmas lights," she whispered as the glow faded. I turned to see that the static had transformed her hair to wreathing seaweed.

"You look a fright," I said. "Do you think you'll be able to sleep?"

"I don't think so. But that's good isn't it? Brides shouldn't be able to sleep the night before their wedding."

"I guess not."

"This is my first time, you know. I never thought it would be out here. You do believe me, don't you?"

"Of course I do."

"But no one else will."

"Who's to say?"

"The Company don't."

"Look, about the Company."

"I don't want to hear about the company."

"Nobody wants to hear about the Company. But I'm obliged to pass on what they said."

"Don't tell me. They're against the idea. They think I could do better." There was that impish writhing in her even now. She scrunched her eyes and sniggered into her glass, looked as if she would fold into a fall. I took her arm to steady her.

"Look, I know it's boring, and all that, but you should know what they said all the same. And then we're straight."

"Oh, go on, then."

"Well, to cut it short. Marriage equals breach of contract, and they'll pursue you over it."

"Surprise."

"They say they're not even contractually bound to bring you back, and if you decide to come back they'll charge you for the trip. It'll cost millions."

"Doesn't matter. I'm not going back. I've got a palace to move into."

"You might change your mind."

"No I won't."

"Nank might change his mind. Later."

"He won't either. And if he does I'll catch a ride with the Indians next year."

"They'll charge you millions."

"So what? Can you imagine what I'd get on the holli rights for all this? *I Married an Urlap*, with Cynthia Slink as Elizabeth Cowper-Delaney."

"Great."

"And introducing Cedric Whimper as her colleague Franz Kortig II."

"Who's Cedric Whimper?"

"How do I know? He sounds like he could do you pretty well, that's all."

"It wouldn't sell. Nobody's interested in the integration question any more. That's all done and dusted."

"Are you kidding? Every girl on Earth wants to know what it's like to do it with an Urlap. I mean *really* know, not just read Sursock or a dumb results table."

"Oh Jesus. Your really mean that, don't you?"

"Uh-huh."

"There is nothing I can say that will change your mind, is there?"

"Nope." She shook her head, brought her hair drifting over her face.

"Well." I took her glass and raised it to the window. "Here's to you, then."

I swigged and gave it back to her to drain.

"Here's to me." She staggered and fell against my outstretched arm as she put her head back, and her head came down upon my shoulder. It stayed there a while, her weaving hair against my cheek. We watched the beauty of the storm's approach: the roiling skirt made purple by the afterglow of evening and the bulge of its mid-levels flashing vast as a universe under the toppling heights. I wondered at the unseen summit probing the stratosphere and thought of the plain-dwelling Uralp buried against it, deep in their holes. The steep black madness of it stilled us both. I felt her shiver at its crashes, and I remembered that holding a girl in a storm is a good and ancient thing.

The storm passed over the city at four hundred kilometres per hour. I discovered this yesterday whilst exchanging pleasantries before the ceremony with the dozen or so guests that waited in Nank's drawing room. The Urlap had been "singing" about it in the copulation pits all night, and now we stood muttering with relief at its passing. Elsewhere that morning there was disorder and destruction; mangled communication towers, collapsed silos, scores of deaths resulting from window failures, so that the marriage seemed a small thing in the shadow of it all. She entered on Nank's arm, Urlap-style, wearing one of the dresses that she'd brought for ceremonials, and I noticed with a tender stifled sob that she had managed to fashion a pillbox hat from the felt separators of our holli cases. The officiating Elder was considerate enough to wear a translator. From my oblique angle I could see past Nank's polished shoulders the tremulous lift of her chin as the words split, flew apart, sometimes joined in click and consonant, were sundered again, familiar and strange: *true, eternity, couple, rejoice, victorious, pride, lust, love*, all this hung in the acrid air of the room. *Go your way into victory, so that at the same time Urlap*, rustled the Elder in conclusion, and the whole thing was done. Nank turned and placed his hand upon her head, she tried vainly to reach above his temple in the Urlap manner, and in this arrangement they slowly made their way out of the room.

So she was an Urlap wife. I had the whole day to think on it. If she had kept herself pure, I knew, she would follow the Urlap tradition and only give herself to him at the rising of the third moon. It is impossible to figure how much delicious torture the priapic Urlap subject themselves to by their conjugal rites, how much whimpering and keening is brought on by this withholding. It is the Urlap tradition to retire from view as soon as the vows are made. They must remain within sight of each other whilst refraining from touching, even the slightest contact, until the astronomical conditions are correct. The ordeal lasts many hours. Failure to observe the tradition is

considered a terrible omen, and no marriage starting
with such a lapse is considered to be properly founded.

Nank, then, would be chirping and pacing with
frustration while she, doubtless, goaded him with coy
glances and suggestive rearrangements of her limbs
beneath that dress which flowed like mercury around
her. This thought drove me back to our quarters, of
which I was now the sole occupant. Sorrowful, I guess.
Failed or beaten, the sensation was not exact.

I spent the afternoon attending to some necessary
matters. I signalled HQ and informed them that the
marriage had taken place, and requested instructions
as to future action. I left a message for her parents in
which I described the wedding in traditional terms,
filling it with as much comforting convention as I
could (details of the dress, a snippet of the homily and
so on). In the afternoon I went into the kitchen and
sprawled on the cold tiles to pull out the stacks of
noodles from the cupboards. I ripped apart every tenth
packet before replacing them, having found nothing.
Later, I lay on a couch and watched the day begin to
close, lulled by the sluggish coagulation of the upper
levels, the sun behind its milky veil unfittingly
peaceful and benign.

When the sun had set and the first moon appeared
over the double hump of the Zelln escarpment, I could
stand it no longer. I went to the kit room, and after
twenty minutes of rummaging through the stored
containers found a mouth mask. Clipping my identity
card to my suit I stepped out of the apartment and
descended to the lobby. There, all was quiet. In a
distant corner, their clicking rising into the high vault,
a group of Urlap, probably a visiting delegation from
the provinces, conversed in a close group. I traversed
the other side of the lobby unnoticed, and the guards
at the door inclined their heads politely as I exited into
the tube hub. They did not turn to notice that I took

the residential quarter tube rather than the usual route
to the ministries. I passed no one in the fifteen
minutes of curling, slow descent to the royal district. I
would not have known what to say if I had been
stopped and challenged. In truth, I had no strategy or
plan, no inkling of destiny.

There is a copulation pit across the street from
Nank's palace, and attached to it is a small *crul* bar
with an open front. Only a few hundred metres from
the tube exit, I went over them with my head tortoised
into my shoulders in anticipation of a blow or grasp.
My arrival at the bar caused the half-dozen occupants
to rise from their tables and crush against the back
wall. There really was some mighty Urlapian terror in
that dingy box. I figured that this place was for the
servants, the cooks and gardeners and so on, who had
never clapped eyes on the human jelly before. I made a
show of putting on my mouth mask, waggling the new
pungent rubber to show its close fit, and took a seat
near the footpath. Look, no disease! was what I meant
by that. Sitting with my back to the interior I heard
the slow return of the customers, the scraping of
reoccupied chairs and the recommencement of the
chattering which I had interrupted. I began to relax.
These were Urlap after all, to flee from an Earthling, or
attack him, would be unsophisticated.

I noticed, after a few minutes, that a small bowl of
crul had been placed beside my elbow by the waiter,
but I made no attempt to drink it. My attention was
fixed upon the palace opposite, its rounded flanks
rising from the road in a series of slopes and plateaux.
The bar overlooked the rear of the building, and above
the roughness of the exterior wall the palace was
almost windowless. But on the third floor, high above
the street, I recognised the intricate workings of
dormitory windows, and by the size of the one most
centrally placed I guessed I had found the main

bedchamber. It was a square of even warm light behind its sanded glass. No movement could be seen within it, not even a shifting in its placid glow. My eyes only left it to search in vain for the rise of the second moon, which I knew must be taking place somewhere behind the palace's old stone.

I thought of Nank and Elizabeth inside that room preparing for the moment of consummation. The patrons of the bar continued to chatter, oblivious to what was soon to take place, the rhythms of their clicks and trills falling into a more restful mode, there was the occasional hollow knocking of humour even, so that I was thankful to have forgotten my translator so as not to be offended by their indifference. I wondered if they would have felt as I did, had they known what I knew. Guessing that the second moon had risen, I set the timer on my V for twenty minutes and, occasionally pulling aside my mouth mask, pretended to sip my *crul*.

What was I expecting to happen? Nothing, I could plainly state, and nothing came. At twenty-five minutes the gold of the window was as flawless as it was when I arrived. No sound emerged from the palace, there was no movement along the wall or across the palace's many smooth facets, and as I sat in the deepening night and felt the eyes of the bar on my back I began to question the wisdom of the whole thing, my presence here.

But then came a tearing of the light. The window opened from its centre to reveal a silhouette – human or Urlap, it was impossible to say. I fought the urge to leap up, afraid of alarming the patrons of the bar again. None of them noticed the opening of the building above them, which had been carried out with furtive quiet. I raised the glass of *crul* to my lips and, blinking through its bitter miasma, watched as the figure looked left and right along the street, then downwards at the sloping palace roofs. Its movement, I now saw, unmistakably human. The head withdrew for a moment, and I thought that I had seen the last of it, that I should have cried out when I had the chance, and I was on the verge of rising for a better view when a leg emerged, and then another. She smoothly lowered herself out of the window to hang on its frame, emerging backwards into the light so that I could see that she was wearing a sort of peignoir which must have been a gift from Nank, sheer enough to show the soft humanity beneath. She dangled there for a moment, like a gymnast preparing for a swing up onto the bars, and then dropped the few feet to the roof below her. This was a narrow slope, perhaps ten feet in length, and she descended along it with the tiptoeing of a child, her hands raised to balance herself.

Now I stood, and heard the crashing of the Urlap behind me as they fled to the back wall. I tore away the mask and cupped my mouth to shout, but hesitated, afraid that she would lose her footing if startled. I watched instead as she paused at the lip of the first roof and then hopped onto the obverse slope of a second, a longer stretch which brought her halfway to the ground. Another silhouette appeared in the window she had escaped from, jerkily Urlapian it flickered against the room's warmth as it sought her out. It became still for a moment as it found her, observed her descent along the roof, and then it withdrew. Lights began to come on elsewhere in the palace.

I shouted: "Elizabeth!" She glanced in my direction and then returned her attention to the edge of the roof below her. Another jump, this time onto a steeper slope that would take her to the top of the exterior wall. Beginning to slide, she flicked herself sideways and bent the higher knee, a skier's turn, and in this

way performed a perfect glissade – oh I almost leapt in
the air at the high style of it – for the entire drop to the
wall's crenelation. Bending to steady herself on a
merlon (a Nankish touch, that), she looked up and
down the street which I was now crossing at a jog.

"What are you doing here?" she shouted.

I could think of no answer. I ran to the base of the
wall and raised my arms. "Jump. I'll catch you."

She laughed. "You'll drop me."

"No I won't. Just jump. We'll be alright."

She sat on the edge of the wall and frowned towards
the ground. I heard a clanging to my left and turned to
see the opening of a postern. The palace guard began
to file through it and assemble on the street.

"Quickly, jump."

She twisted to look up at the window through which
she had fled. The silhouette had returned, motionless
in the frame. She turned to face me and said, with an
uncertain flexing of her shoulders: "There really is no
need. I think everything will be all right."

"For God's sake, jump," I shouted. "There's nothing
they can do if we report this to Exterior Affairs. The
Urlap wouldn't dare do anything if we go diplo on
them. We'll get back to our quarters and signal home
from there."

She raised her eyebrows, softly sighed and pushed
her hips forward to let herself drop.

"That's it! That's it!" I cried.

It was Urlap arms which caught her. The guard
reached over and around me, I was crushed amidst the
fibrous limbs and knocked to the floor. By the time I
had got to my feet they had set her down and locked
arms around her. I saw her tousled hair (garlanded, I
noticed for the first time, with synthetic daisies),
between the heads of her captors which glistened as
toffee apples in the moonlight. They began to move
her away from me, towards the open postern.

"Elizabeth!"

She wriggled in their grip to face me, half-lifted from the floor. Two of the Urlap fell away from the group to bar my progress, clasping my biceps with a cold grip. I struggled forward all the same, ignoring their harsh ticking, dragging the Urlap with me, and when the ranked guard paused to negotiate its way through the narrow gate I freed an arm to reach out to her.

She shook her head. "Don't worry. I just got a bit of a fright, that's all."

"Tell him," I gasped, "tell him to let you go. If he's such a gent he'll listen."

Her head shook again. "I'm going back. Please don't worry."

"You don't have to, you know, you don't have to do any of it."

"I know. But it's what I want."

Well, futility. I saw it all then nice and clear. The guard moved slowly into formation in order to pass through the gate two-by-two. She gave no resistance, standing quietly under the grip of a single hand placed on her shoulder. She was lovely in the moonlight, it must be said, the light and dark of her finely worked and flawless. She stood with her head bowed to wait, and my finger, reaching, found her cheek. When she raised her head towards me I saw the placid smile.

"Elizabeth?"

She nodded only, and responding to a nudge from one of the guard she stepped through the postern. The remainder shuffled after her and the gate was banged shut. I made no attempt to follow, and turned away from the palace without looking back at the window. There was nothing to be gained from meeting Nank's stare, and I had seen in her starlit eyes, those moist eyes grey with chill universal light, the truth in what she'd said.

Andrew Peters *is an Egypt-based financial writer, who has recently started to publish fiction. His short story "In Dogpoo Park" was chosen as Editor's Pick in the Aestas 2016 Short Story Competition run by Fabula Press, and was published in an anthology this year. Some of his flash fiction will also be appearing in the 2017 Fish Anthology, having been chosen in competition.*

Doggerland

Jule Owen

The Pangea is the greatest miracle of ingenuity in recorded human history. It makes all those hysterical twenty-first century predictions of the imminent demise of humans seem as ridiculous as the Aztecs and 2012, and a thousand other superstitious myths of the apocalypse. To be human is to adapt, and the Pangea is the ultimate testament to this.

Sure, a thousand years ago there was war, pestilence, deluge and famine. Forests burned, the Arctic Circle permafrost melted and became nearly eight million square miles of methane-pumping, highly flammable, uninhabitable hell. The great cities of the earth – New York, Alexandria, Ho Chi Minh City, Amsterdam, New Orleans, Bangkok, Hong Kong, Tokyo, Mumbai, Shanghai and Miami – all became curious lakes with tips of broken and abandoned buildings piercing their surface waters. Over nine million species, some 20 billion billion individual animals, became extinct in earth's sixth and greatest mass extinction, more devastating even than the Permian. And most of the eleven billion human beings clinging to the earth were eliminated, leaving only a pathetic, dispersed, lonely cringing million.

But things have been worse. The genetic record of modern humans indicates that, in ancient times past, they were reduced, by some forgotten tragedy, to just 2000 individuals. So, a million people, a thousand years ago, scattered and devastated as they were, were more than enough to get started again.

It is hard to get emotional about it. It is too much to take in, too long ago.

Besides, all this is simply the colossal computer of the universe cranking its unfeeling way through its great program of creation and destruction, refining all the while. There is no doubt that the people of the Pangea are a step forward in evolution, a better version of the human pattern, the most perfect living intelligent product the earth could make.

This is a litany Marsh never questions, a fact so obvious that it is a waste of neural energy to dwell on it.

Any time he wants, he can have a bird's-eye view of the miracle; see the proof with his own eyes. Fly over it in his mind in a way that is so tangible, so much more concrete than anything he ever experiences in the so-called Corporal World in the rooms and corridors of Doggerland.

The Pangea is named, of course, after the supercontinent of the late Paleozoic and early Mesozoic eras. The modern version is an unbroken supercity that covers every available surface of the earth and bridges stretches of water between land masses. If you are so inclined, you can take a single train from Norilsk in Siberia to Puerto Williams in Chile. Someone did it once, too, a few hundred years ago, when these things still seemed novel, or so the Unity reflexively tells him (he has very little memory of his own). The pioneer was a woman called Munoz.

It is Marsh's job to patrol and maintain the rooftops of Doggerland, the administrative and physical section of the Pangea that connects mainland Britain to the Netherlands and Germany. Of course, these old distinctions are anachronistic. The designations Britain and France have roughly the same meaning to a modern Pangean as street names had to twenty-first century humans. It makes little difference whether a Pangean's habitation is rooted on land or the seabed. Many years ago, people cared. There was a certain excitement about living on the sea. People paid more, when people still paid for things, for sea-view apartments, or better still, apartments with windows that were underwater. Doggerland still has thousands of these apartments, but people have covered the windows with digital screens that can show something more interesting than the monotonous, pristine, unchanging dead cobalt blue of the North Sea. Marsh's apartment doesn't have a window, but there is an observational deck, off the main concourse, which does. Hardly anyone visits it.

Or at least, he never does.

Marsh is the director of a large unit. Nominally, it entitles him to a "superior" grade of credit allowance, although, as no one ever discusses these things, he has no idea what the basis for comparison is. Perhaps everyone is a director and everyone's credit grade is superior. It is considered impolite to ask, and he would be in breach of his work contract if he discussed it. So, he never has and he doesn't know.

His unit consists of three hundred servants, AIs and a considerable number of drones. He also has Jade, his companion. She is a tactile hologram who, if he stops to think about it, is technically in his employ, in that he pays for her. But she is not associated with his work and, given the personal nature of the arrangement, he doesn't like to think about the transactional side of things. It makes it seem sordid.

The servants in his unit take care of the day-to-day grunt work, freeing him up to be available for higher-level decision making and to attend managerial meetings with the other human directors in his section. Only humans can be directors. Despite all the discussion about the higher reasoning abilities of AIs, it still takes a human to make the important calls. The endless meetings are tedious, but a necessary and important part of keeping the Pangea running. It is a privilege, he frequently reminds himself, to be invited to attend. As one of his fellow directors once told him, only a human mind could possibly appreciate the nuanced significance of the outcomes of those meetings. An AI, hard-wired for productivity, would never understand the point of them. They would quickly decide they weren't necessary at all.

Marsh's rooms are large, or at least he thinks they are. It is a long time since he's been inside any other rooms and his memory is hazy on the subject. The Unity tells him this is so. There's a bedroom with a large king-size bed and crisp white sheets, changed and laundered regularly by the house servants, featureless robots with limited conversational abilities. There's an ultrasound shower in the en suite and even a bath. The lounge is square, with an expanse of sofa and chairs that can accommodate many guests. In the past Marsh has filled the place up with the holograms of his fellow directors and has thrown dinner parties with Jade as his hostess. He's even had some of his more humanoid servants over. He hasn't done it for a while. Ten years or so, at least. It was something he just lost interest in.

The walls of his windowless apartment are more interesting than any window. They can be anything he wishes. The apartment can be anything he wishes: a desert, a jungle, a temperate forest. It is interesting how, after so many years of so much choice, he has opted for whiteness. White walls, white furniture, space, spareness, emptiness. Even Jade's hair is white, the colour of her eyes blue ice, so pale, her lips, her skin bloodless.

One day, Marsh wakes up and lies awake for a while

staring at the ceiling. He is trying to remember the last time he left his apartment. Doggerland, he remembers, has large, beautiful communal areas, with trees and plants, running water, pools for swimming, saunas, bars, restaurants and numerous entertainments. Yet he cannot remember the last time he ventured out. He looks at Jade, who is sitting passively at the end of the bed. He asks, "Can you remember when I last went to the concourse?"

Jade turns her head to look at him. If she wasn't an AI, he would say she was frowning and looking at him with a mixture of concern and condescension.

"Twenty years, three months, fifteen days," she says.

Twenty years wasn't such a long time. In the lifetime of a Pangea resident, which could now stretch on for five hundred years or so, assuming good maintenance and no unlucky new mutations, it was really a trivial amount of time. The original Marsh, Marsh One, had only lived to ninety before he was considered too broken to repair. Marsh Two had got to one-hundred-and-fifty; Marsh Three had contracted a computer-borne virus concocted by a terrorist touting some obscure nonsense about the natural world. That Marsh had died prematurely at sixty. The current Marsh is only two hundred years old, not even middle-aged, by the predictions of the system. His proper name is Marsh Six, but no one ever calls him that because there is no other Marsh alive anywhere on the Pangea.

There are other names that Marsh has ownership of. This is a peculiar, almost superstitious thing. A throwback to times past that makes him uncomfortable, but nevertheless he is programmed never to forget those names; the Dead Names, the names of all that have had a part in making him, the people he carries around in his genes, but whose names have not been carried on in any living individual in the Pangea and, given the one-for-one replacement policy, never will be. It gives him a peculiar feeling to think about them, an unsettling, unpleasant feeling which travelled with him for days after the Day of the Dead Names, the anniversary set aside for remembering. He finds it hard to imagine them, those hundred and twelve names he has been given. Some people have more, some people have fewer, depending on what has been recorded in the past. They come to him in dreams like a horde of zombies risen from the grave, decomposing, staggering towards him, wanting something from him, wanting life. To him they are sub-human, grasping animal things, rutting, reproducing, eating, defecating, decaying, dying; base and uncouth. It makes him shudder to think about them.

"Is anything wrong?" Jade asks. She is staring at him, still with that look on her face. It irritates him. Her programming has some peculiar quirks. But then, she is not human, he thinks. A human wouldn't look at me like that. But this thought sticks. He tries to remember what it is like to have an ordinary domestic conversation with a human. The conversations with the directors in meetings don't count. They are all strictly business, the strict lexicon of the Pangea administration and in the meeting room, they are all avatars, their faces, their mannerisms strictly calibrated for professional conduct. He searches his mind, trying to remember back to the days of the dinner parties and how the humans who came to his apartment behaved, but he cannot conjure an image. He could search his recorded memory in the system, but then Jade would know he was doing it and would start to speculate about why. She would ask questions.

She is still staring at him.

"I'm going out," he says, finally.

"Out?"

"Yes, I'm going out."

"Do you want me to come with you?"

"No. I do not."

When he is in the corridor, he remembers, it is familiar, but it is not as pristine or spacious as those memories. It is very clean. You could probably eat food off the floor, but it seems dated. He must remember to tell the director in charge of corridors. This passage leads to the concourse. It is the hub of a giant wheel, from which sprout the spokes of walkways leading to hundreds of apartments, just like Marsh's. A central corridor connects the hubs for each section of habitation, stretching the full length of Doggerland, from Britain to mainland Europe, a chain of communal space. He never remembers the concourse being busy exactly, but he is sure that when he visited before, there were other people. But as he steps out of his corridor onto the central platform, there is no one else there. Not a soul. He checks the time, thinking somehow he has managed to get up in the middle of the night, as he has sometimes done before, but it is mid-morning.

The light is strange. He is on the mezzanine level of a vast atrium and high above him there are windows beaming down natural light. He knows those windows. It is his job, after all, his servants' job, to clean and maintain them, but it is a long time since he has seen them corporally. It is a long time – how long? – since he has stood under natural light. It doesn't seem real to him. Exposed, vulnerable, he steps out into the empty space. It is so unnerving he almost turns around and goes back to his apartment, but something, curiosity perhaps, makes him overcome his inclination for the familiar.

The mezzanine has a wide balcony. Lining the inner walls there are shops, restaurants, bars and communal spaces, all totally empty of people. The shops are, after all, some peculiar historical throwback. No one buys anything anymore. No one needs anything. The bars and the restaurants are an excuse to socialize, eating and drinking being an optional process that most people don't bother with except for social situations. Nutrition, energy and hydration requirements are all taken care of by bio-modifications managed by the central AI of the Unity. The Unity also takes care of waste disposal, when required. Eating is meant to be carcinogenic, he remembers. Perhaps that is why the restaurants are empty. He walks around the whole platform and settles his forearms on the rail in the centre, looking down to the ground, or rather, seabed level. All floors are the same: deserted.

But then he looks up, across the gap, into the coffee shop on the other side of the mezzanine. He double-takes.

There is someone there.

He tries not to hurry.

It is a female. Brown-skinned, like him. She looks young, but as everyone is optimized to look twenty-two, appearances are meaningless. The Unity tells him she is in fact four hundred and twenty-seven. She is drinking when he enters the coffee shop. She sees him approach. The cup stops and hovers by her lips, her mouth hanging open.

To steady himself he goes first to the serving counter. The robot servant asks him for his order. He hesitates. It is a long time since he has done this. He looks at the menu. "Espresso?" It comes out as a question, but the robot doesn't seem to notice.

When it is made, he takes his drink over to a table near the woman and starts to sit.

"Won't you join me?" she asks.

He hesitates, his legs squat, his back bent, hovering over his chair. Then he says, "Thank you," and he takes a seat opposite her.

He carefully positions his coffee cup. She has a plate of croissants and rolls and a large milky coffee.

"I hope I'm not interrupting?"

She smiles at him. Perfect white teeth. She has found what he said amusing, but she is not mocking him. He realises she thinks he's deliberately made a joke. Her eyes sparkle. Her face is alive.

"Not at all," she says.

He takes a sip of his drink. It is bitter. There is no sweetener in it. He doesn't like espresso. He doesn't know why he ordered it. "Where is everyone?" he asks.

"For a long time, I wondered that myself. But apparently, this place is not very interesting when you can have anything you want in your own rooms."

"So, why do you come?"

She raises an eyebrow, "Why did you?"

"I asked first."

She smiles again and shrugs, "Habit."

"You come often, then?"

"Every day."

"Are there ever others?"

"Well, there's you, today. But not normally. Not for a long time."

"Why?"

"You tell me. Where have you been?"

"I don't know for sure. In my rooms." He looks confused. "I remember there being more people."

"When? When did you last come here?"

"I can't remember. Twenty years ago. I don't know."

"Why don't you check your recorded memory?"

"I don't like to. It's like I don't trust it. Sorry, I can't explain."

She looks at him. Really looks. Holds his gaze and nods slightly as if she understands and he feels a flush of something he hasn't felt for a lifetime. Comradeship. Connectedness. Sympathy.

"So you don't come to meet people?"

"Oh, I do. I always hope I will see someone; someone I can talk to who isn't a robot or a hologram or an avatar locked in a room."

"When is the last time? Before me, I mean?"

She searches her memory. "A couple of years ago. Every now and then, someone emerges to look around. Like you. They rarely come back, though."

"Why do you come back?"

"It gets me out of my room. And I like to stop off here before I go to the viewing window."

Something ignites deep amongst his dormant synapses. A vague memory.

"A window. I think I've seen it. It's under water."

"Yes. It looks into the sea."

"But there is nothing, is there? It never changes. Just sand and blue water."

"I saw something once."

He knows his expression is wrong. It is showing disbelief. Incredulity. He sees her react. He flushes with shame. "Isn't it all...?"

"Dead?"

"Yes."

"All I know is what I saw. It was so big." She measures the imaginary thing between her thumb and her index finger. "A kind of jellyfish, I think. Beautiful. Pink and blue. Transparent, and it danced in the water. It had tendrils that pulsated with electricity. It floated about right by the window for a full five minutes. They were the happiest five minutes of my entire life. I cannot get it out of my head."

"A jellyfish."

"Yes. I saw a jellyfish."

"That's extraordinary. Did you report it?"

"To whom?"

"The Unity."

"Why?"

"They could... they would..." But what would they do?

"It is dumb, the Unity. It doesn't care. You know that, don't you? It does not feel."

He doesn't know what to say and he feels panic, searching around desperately for something. Then, "Did you see it again?"

"No, never."

"But you go back every day?"

"Yes."

"Why?"

She smiles at him. "Why, in case it comes back, of course."

"But aren't you disappointed when it doesn't?"

"The anticipation, the hope that it might, makes me happy."

"Happy?"

"Come with me," she says. "Come and look."

She doesn't ask him if he wants to finish his coffee.

The observation deck is designed around a vast window in the side of Doggerland. Each section has one. It is connected between levels by a glass lift. In front of the window there's a low long bench. The woman takes a seat in the centre. He sits a little way apart from her, and he looks, as she does, out of the window at the sea.

It is a floor-to-ceiling sheet of blue, dark because of the depth but, given that, remarkably clear. The sea bottom is pristine sand. There are no fish, no plants. Everything is dead.

"What is your name?" he asks, after a while.

"Baker Five," she says. He makes the calculation, and realises she must be nearing her end of use.

He sits with her a while, enjoying her company, although they speak no more. Then a Unity alert comes through telling him he needs to leave for his shift. His servants are doing a flyover of a worn section of roof and he wants to observe for his director's report. He could easily watch a recording but it comes across better if he is there, making observations.

Back in his apartment he enjoys the experience of flying out with his crew of drones. He loves the expanse of the Pangea roof. It fills the view screen fully, the cloudless blue sky beyond it, the merciless sun, the thin atmosphere packed full of greenhouse gases. The whole world's a greenhouse now. They travel along galleys and gutters, swiftly checking the integrity of the external fabric of the building for leaks. The storms from which the Pangea protects its inhabitants are brutal and biblical in scale. They come crashing over the sea out of nowhere and consume the sky, colossal clouds piled like gods spitting lightning, massive twisters, winds that gather funnels of water and dump it miles away. They rip fabric and structures from the exterior of the Pangea, which means it needs to be constantly repaired. Hordes of drones and miniature robots crawl about on the outside in the quiet times and retreat like scurrying insects when the storms whip up.

The next day he goes back to the concourse at the same time, but he doesn't see Baker Five in the restaurant. He goes to the observation deck alone and sits and watches the clean, barren sea. He does this every day, but Baker Five doesn't appear. He tries to contact her via the Unity, but gets the notice "Refreshing", which means, as he had suspected, she has reached her end of use. This ought not to bother him. There will be a Baker Six, after all, who will look and sound identical. And there are hundreds, thousands of beings, human and artificial to talk to, but the idea of Baker Five and her jellyfish has attached to him like a virus, and won't let go. Baker Six may not feel the need to go to the concourse, eat croissants and visit the viewing deck. Baker Six will not remember the jellyfish.

"There was no jellyfish, you know," Jade says.

"What?"

"She could not have seen a jellyfish."

"Because the sea is dead?"

"Because there is no window. It's a screen like the ones here in this apartment. It isn't possible to put a window in a structure this size, this deep in the water. It would break from the pressure."

"It's a screen?" Marsh looks at Jade, incredulous.

"Of course."

"But why the jellyfish?"

"The system probably thought she needed something to keep her mind occupied."

"It made the whole thing up?"

"Yes."

"What is on the outside, then?"

She shrugs. "Who knows?"

"Does the Unity know?"

"Probably, but it won't tell me. Or you."

"Why?"

"It knows best. I shouldn't worry about it."

"But if the window is a screen and the Unity can project anything onto it, would it not populate the sea with animals? It would be more interesting to look at, after all."

Jade hesitates. She never hesitates. It's just a fraction of a fraction of a second, like there has been an error and an instantaneous correction. In that moment, the answer to his own question occurs to him, but he doesn't say it out loud. He doesn't speak, even though he knows the Unity reads his every thought. He is still looking at Jade and she is looking back at him, but there is wariness between them. His thought is this: Because if they make it interesting, I will want to go outside and look for myself.

Later, Marsh is sitting at his terminal, flying virtually with his drone servants along the gullies and channels of the top of the Doggerland complex. He watches the sky and the edges of the roof, where the outer world might be. He tries to negotiate with the Unity to fly a drone off the edge, to see what is there, but receives polite but persistent rebuttals. A thought is all that is required to conjure a virtual version of what he wishes to see, but it irks him that he is not permitted to look for himself.

Later still, he really goes out, takes his corporal self, and walks the corridors to the concourse and the observation deck, still looking, against hope, for Baker Five. He spies the glass lift. Standing inside it, he wonders how long it is since it has been used.

It works perfectly.

He watches the floors go by as the glass box climbs up its shaft and passes by the great glass window on the sea, which he now knows is not a window at all, but a screen; a mirage. When the lift will go no further, he gets out, steps forward towards the screen and slowly seats himself on the long bench. The surface of the water laps up against the glass, or it looks like it does. There's a white glassy undulating lip of water separating the clean blue of the North Sea and the cloudless azure sky. He gazes across the surface of the water, knowing now it's not real, but unable to see it any other way. The sea stretches away to the horizon, empty; no land, structure or lifeforms. His eyes wander to the top of the window / screen and up and beyond to the glass roof of the atrium of the concourse. Through it he can see the sky. Just at that moment a drone whizzes by, one of his own: his servant. He gets to his feet.

His memory must not be as shot and helpless as he thought. A small piece of random knowledge pops in his head. There is an old staircase, built for service and emergencies; built for evacuation. It is through an unmarked door, down a dead-end corridor, off the main concourse. He cannot remember ever climbing stairs before. The movement of making his limbs go up steps is unfamiliar, but his muscles are maintained in peak condition by the Unity and it does not tire him. Ten flights around and around a utilitarian stairwell lead to an innocuous-looking door. Which is locked. Firmly. Like an angry shut mouth, lips firmly pressed together, on the face of the Unity. It does not want him to open the door.

Marsh is a big man, like all Pangean people, bred and engineered to the perfection of the human form; a muscle-bound, broad-chested creature who has never had to use his own strength, but he uses it now. He ploughs his iron shoulders, his weight, his fully optimised energy into the door again and again, like an enraged animal. And he surprises himself because he is very angry. And the door gives. It gives some more. He falls out into the day, tumbles out, thrown by his own force onto the roof of Doggerland.

It is familiar, the solar-energy-conducting black material of the roof, the channels that quickly route the brief torrential rains to a place of capture to be usefully brought into the system of the Pangea, before they can be evaporated by the sun. The tiles are searing hot to the touch. He makes for a shaded part, leans against a wall and raises his gaze. At first, he thinks he must be looking at a nearby island. He edges out from the wall. The soles of his shoes are sticky, melting. He keeps walking, not quite believing, and peers over the edge.

There is no water.

Blown up against Doggerland and stretching forth in every direction as far as the eye can see is sand. He remembers Jade's words: what he saw through the observation deck window was an illusion: a screen. There is no sea. It is all boiled away.

He turns around. On the far horizon is a familiar sight: a colossal funnel of cloud, churning a random path across the landscape, sucking up anything in its path. There is a flash of lightning against the darkening sky. A storm is coming. Drones, his servants, swarm towards him and then disappear down a hatch nearby, taking refuge. Nothing on the roof will survive a storm like that.

So, he sits and waits.

Jule Owen was born and raised in Merseyside and now lives in London. By day she is a practising digital technologist, working on products that involve machine learning and automation, by night she writes stories about future and other worlds.

The Quarterly Review

Reviews by Stephen Theaker, Douglas J. Ogurek, and Rafe McGregor

Douglas J. Ogurek's work has appeared in the BFS Journal, The Literary Review, Morpheus Tales, Gone Lawn, and several anthologies. Douglas's website can be found at www.douglasjogurek.weebly.com.

Rafe McGregor is the author of The Value of Literature, The Architect of Murder, five collections of short fiction, and over one hundred magazine articles, journal papers, and review essays. He lectures at the University of York and can be found online at https://twitter.com/rafemcgregor.

Stephen Theaker is the co-editor of TQF and shares his home with three slightly smaller Theakers.

We don't have a policy on ratings, other than that reviewers use them or not as they prefer.

Books

All Systems Red, by Martha Wells (Tor.com)

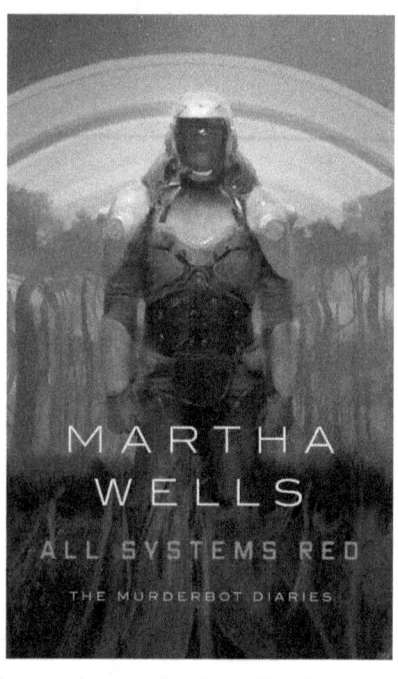

People are using wormholes to travel to distant planets, and since that can be a dangerous business their insurers tend to insist that the expeditions include a so-called murderbot (a SecUnit) to do any necessary killing. They also record every conversation for later data-mining. One of these robots is our protagonist, and since it has hacked the governor module that would normally keep it under control the explorers don't realise how much danger they are in. Luckily for them, the murderbot prefers soap opera to grand guignol. Less luckily, someone or something else has tampered with their equipment and data. When a competing base on the other side of the world goes dark, the murderbot accompanies the scientists on a trip to investigate, while trying to deal with the social anxiety that inevitably results from spending time with people who at any moment could rumble its secrets and have it disassembled. They freak out enough even when seeing it has a humanoid face under its helmet. This is a short, very enjoyable book about an anti-hero who can take a lot of damage and keep on going, who almost despite itself starts putting others ahead of its own interests; a bit like Wolverine or Snake Plissken but with the insecurity that comes from its particular circumstances. Placing a character like that in a terribly dangerous scenario with ruthless villains on the loose and a bunch of decent scientists to protect makes for good reading. The fight scenes are very well worked, and so is the evolution of the robot's relationships with its colleagues/leaseholders. I doubt this'll be the last book I read about this robot. *Stephen Theaker* ★★★★☆

Closet Dreams, by Lisa Tuttle (infinity plus)

Part of the infinity plus singles series, which aim to bring back the feel of buying a vinyl 45, and then liking it so much you would buy the album too. Short stories are the singles, collections the albums. In this case the single has already been a hit, having appeared in *Postscripts*, been shortlisted for a Bram Stoker Award, and and won the International Horror Guild Award. It's the

chilling story told by a young woman, who says, "Something terrible happened to me when I was a little girl." Held captive in a small closet by an abductor, she describes the miraculous escape that baffled her family and the police. It's not a long story, so it's hard to say much more without giving too much away, but it certainly achieved the goal of making me want to read more by the same author. *Stephen Theaker* ★★★★☆

Final Girls, by Mira Grant (Subterranean Press)

Virtual reality horror scenarios are being used to heal family wounds. Sisters like Kim and Diane go in hating each other, and their relationships are reforged in the fire of being hunted by by a serial killer. A journalist, Esther Hoffman, comes to investigate the process, concerned by the power of such false memories, a deeply personal concern because of what happened to her father

when she was young. Unfortunately her visit coincides with that of an industrial spy and so her trip into virtual reality becomes even more horrific than expected. It's a good novella that explores the interplay between memories and emotions and relationships and asks whether, if we could tweak those things to make them better, we should. The horror scenes are frightening enough to convince the reader that going through them would have the claimed effect. *Stephen Theaker* ★★★★☆

Proof of Concept, by Gwyneth Jones (Tor.com)

Kir is a young woman with an AI embedded in her head, and this was done by her mother, Margrethe Patel, who adopted her precisely for this purpose. Kir was born in one of the heavily irrradiated and ever-growing Dead Zones that cover the Earth while most people cram into overcrowded dictatorial Hives. Mum

trained her as a
scientist, while touring
the world so that people
could pay for the use of
her onboard computer,
and now they have gone
deep underground on
the Needle Voyager
mission, in a massive
cavern deep under the
Giewont mountain in
Poland. There are
habitats on Mars and
the Moon, but the
future is not looking
great for humanity, and
so the hope is that

Margrethe and her team can find a way out.
Unfortunately part of the deal is that the scientists are
joined in the base by the irritating future equivalent of
YouTubers, and as events unfold Kir's trust in her
mother is put under increasing stress. Short novels are
one of my favourite things, and at 140pp this hits the
sweet spot. Yet even I was wondering, with sixteen
minutes of reading to go, how it could possibly wrap
up all the (personal, political and criminal) plotlines
without at least a few hundred pages more. Somehow
it does. There's room for sequels, and people may be
surprised by the suddenness of the ending, but no one
could complain that they didn't get enough story. And
it's an inventive story with strong characterisation. It's
impossible not to sympathise with the difficult
situation in which Kir finds herself, to worry for her as
she sneaks out of the base to chill out in the black
abyss, or to keep one's fingers crossed as she takes her
first tentative steps towards a romantic relationship.
Stephen Theaker ★★★★☆

Working for Bigfoot, by Jim Butcher (Subterranean Press)

This collection of three short stories seems like a handy introduction to the Dresden Files, a highly successful series of novels about the work of Harry Dresden, a professional magician. These tales take place at different points in his life, Harry being hired three times by a bigfoot with the brilliant name Strength of a River in His Shoulders, to look in on his half-human son, Irwin

Pounder – a scion, as they are known. Although these stories have very different sources – "B Is for Bigfoot" first appeared in a book for young readers (*Under My Hat: Tales From the Cauldron*), while "Bigfoot on Campus" debuted in a book of erotica (*Hex Appeal*) – there's no difference in tone or style, just in content. The last story is especially steamy, but not inappropriately so given that the young half-bigfoot is by then the right age for such matters. It's clear from these stories why the character of Harry Dresden is so popular: he's very capable and reliable, and the same goes for the writing. It reminded of the Jack Reacher books I've read, but with all the fantastical elements that are so sadly missing from the thrillers of Lee Childs. A good little book. *Stephen Theaker* ★★★☆☆

Comics

I Hate Fairyland, Vol. 1: Madly Ever After, by Skottie Young (Image Comics)

Imagine if Dorothy was totally rubbish at quests, got stuck in Oz for twenty-seven years, and it drove her around the bend. That's what happened to Gertrude, much to the dismay and misfortune of everyone in Fairyland. This book collects the first five issues of the series. When Gertrude first arrived as a six-year-old girl, good queen Cloudia told her that there was a door back to her world, and she just needed to find the key, "a quest that should only take two shakes of a bogglezig". The girl sets off with greenfly guide Larrigon Wentsworth III and a map of all the known lands, but never finds her way out. Years later, after Gertrude blows out the brains of the moon and shoots down the stars, the queen has had enough, and starts looking for a way to be rid of the troublesome brat. The rules don't allow her to harm any guest of Fairyland, but there's nothing to stop her hiring someone else to do it. This is a fun, raucous, ultraviolent spoof of books like *The Wonderful Wizard of Oz*. Whereas Catherynne Valente's similarly inspired (in both senses) *The Girl*

'A candy-colored and vicious delight, and always dangerously funny.' ~Neil Gaiman

I HATE FAIRYLAND

SKOTTIE YOUNG

Volume One:
MADLY EVER AFTER

Who Circumnavigated Fairyland in a Ship of Her Own Making tried to reinvent the genre for modern girls, this comic overinflates it till it bursts, leaving bloody entrails everywhere. On Comixology it is rated 17+, but presumably that's for the over the top ridiculous cartoon violence (the moon getting its brains blasted out, the girl eating mushroom people, that kind of thing), and I think it would appeal much more to younger teenagers. It's bright, quick-paced, and appealingly grotesque, and I certainly enjoyed it. *Stephen Theaker* ★★★★☆

Michael Turner's Soulfire: Omnibus 1, by Michael Turner, J.T. Krul, Marcus To and chums (Aspen Comics)

Mal is a teenage boy in the year 2211 who is, as he will find out, a chosen one, the bearer of a spirit that has moved through many lives in preparation for its ultimate destiny. A flying woman with black speech balloons comes to kill him, while another winged woman, Grace, comes to rescue him, and while a giant robot dragon attacks his home city Grace whisks him away, to meet mystics  who can train him to use his powers, and then to other allies in their fight against the evil Rainier and his soldiers. He's a bad guy who survived the end of the last age of magic by embracing technology, and now that magic is on the rise again he is ready to combine the two to ensure his dominance. Luckily Mal has a pair of excellent friends in Sonia and PJ, who have got his back in all this and are willing to follow him way out of their depth.

This is not the kind of comic I usually read, but I can rarely resist a five hundred page omnibus or a comics Humble Bundle and this combined both. It turned out to be a pleasant surprise, very much in the vein of the *Final Fantasy* games. It shares some contributors with Top Cow's *The Darkness*, and there are plenty of pin-up pages of beautiful women, but it's not as sleazy or grotesque as I found *The Darkness* to be (see TQF41 for the review). It would actually be fairly suitable for a young teen. The publisher Aspen is planning to add age ratings to their comics, which has provoked some dismay, but it's possible that, rather that warning children off mature content, their goal is to alert school librarians and parents to the fact that they are publishing books that are suitable for children and that children would like.

It's a simple story told quite well. The experienced Jeph Loeb writes the earlier issues, with J.T. Krul then taking over. Michael Turner draws most of Volume One (the first ten issues collected here), and gets a story credit on them, while Marcus To, whose appealing style suits the story a bit better, takes over on pencils for Volume Two (the next nine issues). It's light, frothy nonsense, and I wouldn't recommend it to our more serious readers, but it was a nice way to spend a few hours. It's colourful and pretty: many scenes take place by the ocean, and the blues of the seas and the sky and the exotic locales give it something of a holiday feel. Like Laura Allred's work on *Madman*, Beth Sotelo's colours and effects in Volume Two are so good that they become a reason to read the comic in their own right. I loved Grace's shimmering Star Trek teleporter hair. *Stephen Theaker*
★★★☆☆

Events

Eastercon 2017: Innominate

I only attended for two days of this four-day convention, Saturday and Monday. It took place in Birmingham, at a hotel close to the NEC, near enough for me to travel to in an hour or so on public transport, so I had bought a full membership fairly early on without knowing whether I would be free or not. My daughter and I attended on Saturday. I bought her a one-day ticket at a very reasonable rate. She was interested in attending a talk on manga and anime, and a session on painting alien worlds, and enjoyed them both. We also watched the BSFA awards, which were good, convivial fun, and then the first episode of *Doctor Who* season ten, which was shown on three huge screens in the main events room.

My daughter enjoyed herself enough to recommend the event to my younger daughter, my wife, and the two children of my co-editor, so they all came with us on the Monday. Upon arriving we had the nice surprise of discovering that my older daughter's painting from the Saturday session had won a prize in the children's art show, which got the day off to a great start. It was a banner day too for my younger daughter, who for the very first time in her life, after being asked for her name, had someone recognise it and say, "Oh, like Telzey Amberdon."

That day we attended hair-braiding and journal

decoration sessions, which were interesting, even for those of us without hair or journals (the hair I lost long ago; the journal I gave away to a little girl who didn't have her own). Between the two workshops we attended the closing ceremony, which must have been an odd experience for the four members of our group who had only arrived an hour and a half before.

Not staying at the hotel overnight, only attending a couple of panels, not being there for the full four days, and not really talking to anyone in the bar, I suppose most people would say I didn't properly get stuck into the convention, but I'd still say it was my favourite convention experience yet. A few years ago I said to an occasional TQF contributor that I didn't really like conventions. He told me that perhaps I had been going to the wrong ones, and after this weekend I think he may have been right.

On the surface this convention was almost completely indistinguishable from the last one I attended in York (my favourite convention before this one), but a few small and significant differences emerged over the couple of days. The strand of events for children was one. (If we'd realised there was a Lego Minifigure event on Sunday we'd have gone on that day too.) It also seemed to have more fans as opposed to career-orientated writers (something at least one writer has grumbled about). And we didn't hear anyone bellowing across the convention rooms like territorial wildebeests.

Course, my experience of other cons is probably coloured to some extent that I went there to present various reports to the AGMs, and watch the awards I'd administered play out, appear on panels a couple of times, and one time be the secretary and treasurer for the whole bleeding thing, whereas Eastercon was pure relaxation, nothing to do except listen to clever people talk about things (Aliette de Bodard was a standout contributor to both panels I attended) or watch the children get on with fun and creative activities.

Best of all, there were plenty of places to sit when nothing was happening. Sofas everywhere, a quiet room, a fan lounge; it really contrasted well with all the times I've been at conventions and struggled to find somewhere to sit and read my new books. There was no goody bag, and no convention souvenir book, two things some attendees of other cons care very deeply about, but I wasn't at all bothered by their absence. The daily newsletters about convention occurrences were great fun.

If Eastercon returns to Birmingham we'll definitely go again, and I think we enjoyed it enough that we could even be tempted a bit further afield. *Stephen Theaker* ★★★★☆

Into the Unknown: a Journey Through Science Fiction, curated by Patrick Gyger (Barbican)

This exhibition, billed as "the genre-defining exhibition of art, design, film & literature", began running at the Barbican on June 3 (the day the TQF co-editors and their families attended), and will be open until 1 September 2017. It was announced in 2016, and I had been looking forward to it ever  since, but in the event it was, despite some remarkable exhibits, a bit of a disappointment. Part of that can perhaps be laid at the tickets, which promise three parts, but only the first was the exhibition proper, and there wasn't very much of it.

The items in the main section included books (not all classics, or valuable editions – it was peculiar to see books I own under glass), magazines, short films (including one written by an AI, the actors gamely trying to find the truth in its words), spectacular model space guns, spaceships, space stations and spacesuits (including John Hurt's from *Alien*, which was amazing to see, though one might doubt its provenance seeing as no hole had been burnt in the faceplate).

The problem is that these are cramped into a very small space, so much so that we were told to carry our backpacks rather than wear them. It would have definitely have had more impact had the items been spaced out more – for example, few in our party even noticed the robot from *Interstellar*, which would have made a formidable exhibit on a plinth of its own, lurking in the shade of Twiki from *Buck Rogers in the 25th Century* and the showier robots from *Lost in Space* and *I, Robot*. Godzilla heads are only visible from a distance, and like many items can only be seen from one side.

The second part is a film, into which only a dozen or so people could enter at a time, leading to queues – odd for a booked event at which the numbers present during any given time slot should have been fairly predictable. (This may well have been sorted out since that first day of opening.) The third part is a robot that spins around shining a light that seems intended to create patterns, giving a sense of artificial intelligence. I spent most of that exhibit worrying about whether the children would tear the paper sheets that surrounded the robot. There is also a selection of sf video games like *Half-Life 2*, and music from people like Tangerine Dream, accessible to the public as well as those attending the exhibition.

"Genre-defining" is a big thing to ask of an exhibition. It is however a pleasant look through the nice collection of a wealthy chap, but one suspects that many visitors will have quite interesting collections of their own, albeit gathered at rather less cost. It's definitely worth a look if you are in London, but overall we didn't feel it had been worth the special trip we made to see it. It was small compared to things like the Doctor Who Experience, and infinitesimal compared to the Warner Brothers Harry Potter tour.

So plan to take your time, don't hurry through, watch the short films and make the most of it all, and perhaps time your visit so that it can include the events and special screenings taking place to tie in with the exhibition's run. Those interested in the exhibition but unable to visit should note that the catalogue is an impressive hardback book, and is available from the Barbican's online shop. *Stephen Theaker* ★★★☆☆

Films

Alien: Covenant, by John Logan and Dante Harper (Twentieth Century Fox et al.)

Scott forgets female leads and the human species in a strange sequel.

Alien: Covenant is the second in a proposed trilogy of prequels to Ridley Scott's *Alien* (1979), following *Prometheus* (2012), which was also directed by Scott and reviewed for TQF by myself, Howard Watts, and Jacob Edwards. The titles of the prequel trilogy have been selected by the spaceships whose stories they tell and the story of the *Covenant* is set ten years after the disappearance of the *Prometheus*. The *Covenant* is en route to Origae-6, a distant planet designated for human colonisation, and is carrying several thousand settlers and embryos and a small crew, all of whom are in stasis with the exception of the ship's synthetic, Walter (Michael Fassbender). The ship is caught in a neutrino blast, which kills the captain and prematurely wakens the crew.

The captain's loss proves significant for two reasons: it introduces his widow, Daniels Branson (Katherine Waterston), who will turn out to be the only human character to make full use of her agency, and it places the second in command, Christopher Oram (Billy Crudup), in charge. Oram is not cut out for his unplanned promotion and makes a series of disastrous decisions, beginning with a diversion to investigate a signal that appears to provide evidence of a human presence on a nearby planet. The signal, as anyone who has watched *Prometheus* will realise, is from Elizabeth Shaw (Noomi Rapace), the sole survivor of the doomed mission to find the origins of human life.

Oram makes another poor judgement call in taking Daniels, who – like Ellen Ripley (Sigourney Weaver) before her – is a third officer turned deputy, with him in the expeditionary force. The first sign of alien trouble occurs about thirty minutes into the film, when one of the crew is infected by spores. These spores and the particular species of alien that will hatch from them are new, but viewers of the series know that something nasty is coming and will not be disappointed by the eye-watering, gut-wrenching gore that ensues. Up to this point, *Alien: Covenant* follows the pattern of *Prometheus* very closely: two spaceships with command problems, two over-confident expeditions to an unknown planet, the infection of two crew members in each expedition – all of which set the scene for an exciting complication, crisis, and climax. Shortly after the emergence of the first aliens from their human hosts, however, the film makes a radical departure from both the initial prequel and the series as a whole.

No sooner has the first alien gone on the rampage, than it is revealed that Shaw is dead and that the sole survivor of the *Prometheus* is David (also Michael Fassbender), the sinister, secretive synthetic with a Peter O'Toole fixation. *Prometheus* ended with Shaw and a badly-damaged David on their way to the planet of the Engineers, the mysterious creators of human life, which is where the crew of the *Covenant* meet David. Curiously, the characters, plot, and themes of the previous film are all handled with complete anti-climax: Shaw is dead, the Engineers have suffered an apocalypse, and no one cares about the origins of humanity anymore. The last of these is especially strange because *Alien: Covenant* begins with a short scene in which billionaire Peter Weyland (Guy Pearce), who funded the *Prometheus* mission, tries to convince David that humanity cannot be an accidental result of the process of evolution. The conceptual unity in the second prequel is provided by creation rather than origin and David has become obsessed with creating life himself.

The *Alien* quartet was dominated by Ripley, the calm, cool, and collected warrior queen who repeatedly saved humankind from the alien menace. *Prometheus* appeared to be setting up Shaw to take over as she proved herself every bit as tough and resourceful as her predecessor/successor. *Alien: Covenant* makes a half-hearted attempt to do the same with Daniels, but Waterston doesn't have the presence of either Weaver or Rapace and – in fairness – receives much less screen time. Fassbender, playing both David and Walter, becomes the most familiar face and dominates the film with crucial roles in the first and last scenes as well as a great deal of what comes in between. In fact, it is not just a strong female lead that is missing in this instalment, but humankind itself and the human beings in *Alien: Covenant* are very far down the food chain. As a sequel to *Prometheus*, this is a *non sequitur*, but as a standalone film set in the *Alien* universe it provides all the thrills and chills one expects from the franchise. *Rafe McGregor* ★★★☆☆

Guardians of the Galaxy, Vol. 2, by James Gunn (Marvel Studios)

The writer of the slightly shocking (but mostly fun) video game *Lollipop Chainsaw* seemed a brave choice to direct a family-friendly space blockbuster, but as so often seems to have been the case Marvel were rewarded for their confidence, the first *Guardians of the Galaxy* being very entertaining, with lots of jokes, a likeable bunch of leads, and a vibrant corner of the Marvel universe to play in. Now the same director and the same cast are back for Vol. 2, thus named for the second Awesome Mix tape that Peter Quill, Star-Lord, received at the end of the first film. Music again plays an important role in the film: the opening sequence shows us Baby Groot trying to dance to ELO's *Mr Blue Sky* while his colleagues battle a space monster in the background, for example. Unusually for a super-hero

movie, this film doesn't set up an ultimate villain right away. It's refreshing for a blockbuster film to have the confidence to do that, knowing our attention won't drift because we're happy to hang out with these characters even if they're just getting into everyday (for them) scrapes and getting to know long-lost family members. Kurt Russell appears as Ego, though Marvel readers will know there's usually a few more words in that name. It's a very pleasant film, just like its predecesor, again with plenty of laughs, though it perhaps missteps a little in not giving as many of them to Star-Lord this time – if Chris Pratt is starring in your space comedy, you need to give him a handful of jokes, even when the focus is mainly on what makes him unhappy. My overriding memory of the film is how beautifully colourful it is. When so many super-hero films of the past have been painted in shades of black, that makes a big impression. *Stephen Theaker*
★★★☆☆

It Comes at Night, by Trey Edward Shults (A24 et al.)

Uncertainty and mistrust take the lead in post-apocalyptic realism at its best.

A sickness is on the loose. It kills quickly. Paul, Sarah, son Travis and dog Stanley hide out in an austere home within the woods. Though they've seen the toll the disease can take, they have no idea of the extent to which it has affected the world. And it seems like something else could be lurking out there. Then another desperate family (Will, Kim and young son Andrew) enters the home. Everyone hopes for a mutually beneficial relationship. Alas, this is a horror movie.

It Comes at Night, written and directed by Trey Edward Shults, is a believable portrayal of what happens when two families, both intent on survival and burdened by mistrust, come together in the midst of an indeterminate threat. The film combines the stripped-down, post-apocalyptic feel of *The Road* (2009), the backwoods locale and defensive paranoia of *The Walking Dead* (2010–present), the intimacy of *Signs* (2002), and the tension and desperation of *Breaking Bad* (2008–2013).

It Comes at Night relies heavily on the unknown to build tension. For instance, the film reveals very little character backstory – it doesn't even divulge their last names – because in this world of uncertainty and immediacy, the past carries little value. More than once, the camera focuses on a frightened Travis as he looks into the forest. What is he seeing? Travis's foreboding dreams and the many instances of light

moving through darkness enhance the effect. Additionally, Shults keeps tossing in wrinkles to keep Paul (and the viewer) unsure of his guests' true motivations.

Worth highlighting is Kelvin Harrison Jr's portrayal of an awkward teen struggling in extraordinary circumstances. Travis eavesdrops on the home's occupants, tries to please a severe, though caring father, and deals with a crush on Kim (a subtlety that a less thoughtful film would skip).

Shults, perhaps taking a page from the brilliant horror film *It Follows* (2014), was wise to insert the word "It" in the title of his film. The pronoun underscores the film's ambiguity. What, exactly, is "It"?

Don't expect to see a lot of "the enemy" in this film, but do remember: some of the most frightening horror films in the last couple decades have employed that very strategy. So if you, like me, delight in films like *The Blair Witch Project* (1999) or *Paranormal Activity* (2007), then you're going to enjoy this one. *Douglas J. Ogurek* ★★★★★

The Mummy, by David Koepp, Christopher McQuarrie and Dylan Kussman (Universal Pictures et al.)

Just leave your brain at the door and enjoy it.

When Tom Cruise takes on a role, no matter what it is, he's going to put his all into it – his characters are believable. In less capable hands, *The Mummy*, directed by Alex Kurtzman, could have been lifeless. Instead, we get a likable protagonist who smiles and sprints his way through (as Cruise so often does) a solid action film wrapped in all the creepy-crawlies, monsters, grand displays of destruction, and narrow escapes for which the most entertaining entries in the Mummy canon are known.

Adventure-seeking American soldier Nick Morton (Cruise) has a weakness for treasure hunting. He has zero interest in the cultural/historical value of the "antiquities" he seeks. So when he and fellow soldier Chris Vail (Jake Johnson) unwittingly discover the crypt of mummified Egyptian princess/murderer Ahmanet (Sofia Boutella) in northern Iraq, they're only interested in the valuables that surround it. But bossy archeologist Dr Jenny Halsey (Annabelle Wallis), a sexual conquest of Morton's, understands the momentousness of the find. Alas, the crypt isn't so much a burial site as it is a prison for Ahmanet, who made a pact with Egyptian god of disorder and violence Set, then killed her entire family so that she would gain power. Nice lady. The trio sets out to move the mummy to London. Mistake. Ahmanet chooses Morton to be the vessel for the return of Set, with whom she will take over the world.

Morton and Halsey, in their quest to stop Ahmanet – Morton refers to her as "the chick in the box" – confront a series of challenges ranging from an underwater chase featuring the reanimated corpses of Crusaders to a massive sandstorm in the middle of modern-day London. Morton also deals with an internal struggle – is he a completely self-absorbed a-hole or is he willing to make sacrifices for Halsey and others?

Russell Crowe's professorial Dr Jekyll

brings an amusingly unnecessary element to the film. Not only does Jekyll inject himself with a giant hypodermic to keep his monster at bay, but he also makes certain to show everyone in the room. The critics scoff, but the aficionados of grandiosity rejoice. And though this Jekyll has vowed to protect the world by eliminating evil, we all know he has a dark side. This is the type of film that demands it comes out.

To those who were disappointed in the film, one must ask – what did you expect? An Oscar-worthy drama? A groundbreaking fantasy film? What I expected was action, silliness, and the Cruise charisma. And that's what I got. *Douglas J. Ogurek*
★★★★☆

Pirates of the Caribbean: Dead Men Tell No Tales, by Jeff Nathanson (Walt Disney et al.)

Shallow content, deep fun.

Seeing a Pirates of the Caribbean (POTC) film is kind of like spending time at an all-inclusive tropical resort – you don't have to think, there are lots of drunken antics, and you walk away with a smile on your face. In the series' fifth instalment, directed by Joachim Rønning and Espen Sandberg, the party continues.

Dead Men Tell No Tales offers no profound life lesson. The bickering young lovers and comic book goal (i.e. find Poseidon's trident) are shameless echoes of the previous films and the talk of maps and stars grows tedious. However, after indulging in the film's strengths, the viewer who doesn't need a serious film to be entertained can brush aside these shortcomings with all the nonchalance of Captain Jack Sparrow (Johnny Depp).

Sparrow at the Crux
Every major player (i.e. Captain Salazar, the British

Empire, Royal Navy sailor Henry Turner, horologist (listen for the pirate banter on this one) Carina Smyth, and Captain Barbossa) is intertwined with Jack Sparrow.

Chief protagonist Henry wishes to use Sparrow's magic compass to lift the curse that has indentured his father Will (Orlando Bloom) to servitude on a ghost

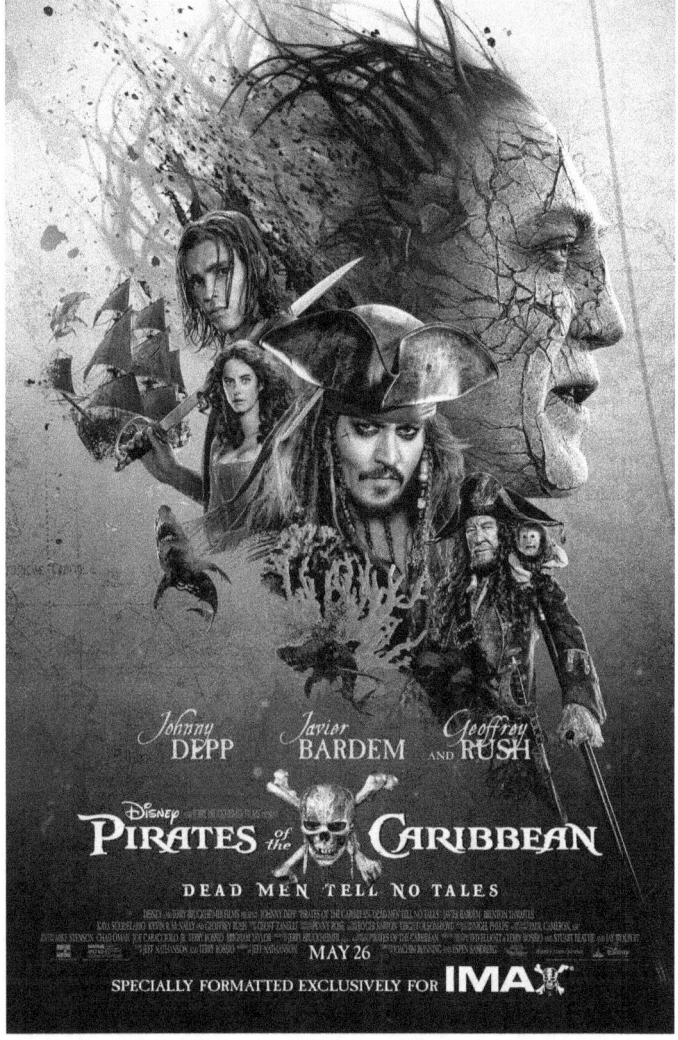

ship. Primary antagonist Captain Salazar (aka "Butcher of the Sea"), played superbly by Javier Bardem, wants not only to unleash the curse that renders him and his crew ghosts, but also to kill Sparrow, who he blames for this misfortune. The power-hungry Salazar takes rasping breaths and his hair constantly undulates as if underwater. "Every time that I'll stamp my sword," he tells one adversary, "one man of your crew will die." And Salazar's ship rears up animal-like before slamming down on its victims.

Action and Eccentricity

The two-and-a-half hour escape that is *Dead Men Tell No Tales* immerses the viewer in lighthearted entertainment: humour, drama, a bit of horror, special effects, beautiful scenery, an entertaining villain, and that adventurous score. But that's all on top of the two strengths that have propelled the POTC franchise: over the top action scenes, and the sometimes (physically and mentally) bumbling, sometimes graceful Captain Jack Sparrow.

Among the key action sequences are an escape from a botched robbery, a diverted execution, and, most gloriously absurd, an attempt to outrow a group of zombie sharks and pirate ghosts who run on water. Often, Sparrow's clumsiness transforms into extraordinary acts of agility. When the film goes slo-mo at key moments, resist the temptation to roll your eyes, and instead just cheer! Yes, a zombie shark jumping over Sparrow and Henry's rowboat is completely pointless, but it underscores the schoolboy spirit of the entire film.

Jack Sparrow, with his swaying movements and rum-infused, yet snappy commentary, secures his spot among the most engaging characters in the contemporary action-fantasy genre. This time, he seduces a politician's wife, falls asleep (standing and pantless) while someone talks to him, fights while attached to a board, and asks his crew members to pay a tribute as *they're* saving *him*. And what other character would tell zombie sharks to "shoo" while flapping a hand at them?

Justified Extravagance
Like all the gems in the POTC treasure chest, *Dead Men Tell No Tales* recognises itself for what it is: a high-action, high-special effects film that isn't overly serious.

Admittedly, I watched this one in a "4DX" theatre replete with moving seats, fog, flashing lights, and sprays of water. But wouldn't Captain Jack Sparrow applaud such extravagance? With the pirate Sparrow, overboard is the way to go. *Douglas J. Ogurek*
★★★★☆

Prometheus, by Jon Spaihts and Damon Lindelof (Twentieth Century Fox et al.)

Scott sacrifices the superficial to the substantive in disappointing prequel.

Sequels and more recently prequels constitute something of a genre of their own in that the play between similarity and difference is at least as important as the director's inventiveness and imaginativeness. Viewers familiar with any one of the *Alien* quartet expect to see gut-wrenching body horror and a gutsy heroine who overcomes adversity, but will be content with neither a re-run of Kane's exploding chest nor a mere replication of Ripley. The demand for resemblance without replication is exacerbated in *Prometheus*, which is both a prequel to the quartet and a prequel to the remaining pair of prequels in the prequel trilogy. One of the concerns of the quartet was the opposition of the capitalist imperative to what one might call basic human values or the more charitable of the religious virtues. Some of the trouble in *Alien* was caused by the profit motive and all of the trouble in the rest of the series was caused by the military-industrial complex's interest in capturing a live alien to create yet another weapon of mass destruction. In this respect, *Prometheus* takes the series to new heights because the quest around which the narrative revolves, the search for the origin of human life, is completely commercial. The venture is not only sponsored by the Weyland Corporation, but undertaken at the whim of its owner and commanded by his representative, Meredith Vickers (Charlize Theron), who treats the *Prometheus*'s captain like a lackey and is openly contemptuous of the scientist passengers.

The new Ripley, Elizabeth Shaw (Noomi Rapace), is one of those scientists and she is responsible for identifying a series of star maps that apparently guide humanity to the planet where our creators, the Engineers, live. Shaw considers the map an invitation to meet our makers and the Weyland Corporation considers it a source of profit for the company and personal gain for an influential board member. Once the *Prometheus* arrives at its destination, the scientific mission begins, albeit very much under the thumb of Vickers and with the corporation's android, David

(Michael Fassbender), clearly having been programmed to pursue an agenda that belongs to neither Vickers nor Shaw. It is at the point of touchdown that the emphasis of the film switches from the superficial story of discovery to a substantive exploration of the human infatuation with genesis. Underlying the literal quest for the origin of human life is a reverence for the species, creature, or being that created humanity and Scott succeeds in capturing the combination of intense curiosity and naïve optimism that drive so many adopted children to seek out their biological parents and so many of the rest of us to investigate our family trees at great financial and emotional cost. The star map *must* be an invitation rather than a trap, there *can't* be any need for the landing party to arm or protect themselves, and the Engineers *must* be benevolent towards their creations. If these assumptions were true, the play of similarity and difference would resemble Stanley Kubrick's *2001: A Space Odyssey* (1968) rather than the *Alien* quartet, and they are quickly revealed for what they are – astonishingly naïve.

The problem for the film is that in exploring this obsession with origins, an exploration that is mirrored by the prequel trilogy's apparent concern with the origins of the species after which the quartet is named, Scott sacrifices the story's suspension of disbelief in its entirety. The result is a film of two parts, the first third plausible and full of suspense and the rest theme-driven to the extent that the plot holes gape as wide as the inevitably self-administered hole in Shaw's stomach. Neither of these two gaping wounds has any recognisable effect: the plot picks up a frenetic pace that Shaw has no trouble matching once she has stapled her stomach shut. I have been generous in my rating on the basis that Scott has not only chosen a highly significant theme for the film, but that his analysis of humankind's origin fetish is serious and sophisticated. I may, however, have been overly generous because Scott provided ample evidence of his ability to pose philosophical questions while maintaining narrative credibility in his first three films: *The Duellists* (1977), *Alien* (1979), and *Blade Runner* (1982). *Prometheus* is his twentieth outing as director and, as such, viewers familiar with his work will expect more. In a word, disappointing, but not disappointing enough to put me off seeing the next prequel. *Rafe McGregor* ★★★☆☆

Wonder Woman, by Allan Heinberg (Warner Bros et al.)

Resolutely she enters the fray.

Finally, a female has joined the contemporary pantheon of high-profile cinematic superheroes... not as a peripheral wisecracking vixen or troubled outcast, but rather as an ass-kicking, yet empathetic lead.

Wonder Woman is tearing up the charts – fourth highest opening weekend for a solo superhero origin film, and the highest-grossing opening weekend for a female-directed (Patty Jenkins) film – with good reason.

Using her shield, sword, magic rope, and physical prowess, Diana/Wonder Woman (Gal Gadot) gracefully dispatches the bad guys. When the film grandiosely portrays Diana in full superhero poise with hair blowing, one can't help but feel exhilarated by the immense physical and moral power of this protagonist.

The "fish out of water" story is told in frame format, with a present day Diana reflecting on her escapades. American spy/pilot Steve Trevor (Chris Pine) inadvertently discovers the beautiful Paradise Island and its all-female warrior inhabitants, including

Diana. When Trevor tells her of the atrocities of the
"war to end all wars", Diana, convinced that Ares is
responsible, sets off with Trevor to the front. She
hopes to kill the god of war and therefore bring the
battle to an end. Trevor, eager to get back to his
superiors, goes along with it. So begins a burgeoning
co-attraction, an exploration of evil and forgiveness,

an opus on women's empowerment, and an irresistible action film featuring one of the most versatile superheroes to date – Wonder Woman can just as easily bash through a brick wall as she can pull off stupefying gymnastic feats.

Never mind that Diana really has no weaknesses and that the villains are one-dimensional. Even more admirable than Diana's ability to plough through the enemy is her unabashed approach to a misogynistic London. She is not afraid to wear what she wants, speak her mind, and most important, to *do something* in the face of injustice.

Each of the two main characters' vastly different world views helps shape that of the other. Diana, raised on an island cut off from the rest of the world, is willing to drop everything to help those in need and harbours no reservations about walking the streets in her conspicuous battle regalia replete with sword and shield. The war-wise Trevor, on the other hand, understands that achieving the ultimate goal sometimes requires tact and covertness.

The spectacle that is *Wonder Woman* keeps the viewer engaged from start to finish. It's also inspirational as an artistic achievement. Lately, when I want to take a project to the next level, I've been asking myself, "How can I Wonder Woman this?" *Douglas J. Ogurek* ★★★★★

Music

Humanz (Deluxe), by Gorillaz (Parlophone)

The Gorillaz have produced a series of innovative, experimental and listener-friendly albums, and being cartoon characters has undoubtedly helped, freeing them from many of the expectations and audience-imposed boundaries that often plague bands. Think of the pushback to Radiohead going electronic on *Kid A* or to David Bowie dabbling in jungle on the underrated *Earthling*. All we expect from Gorillaz is that they will give us something new every time – new collaborators, new sounds, new approaches – and that's exactly what we get from them on *Humanz*. It's like a top twenty from the future, a stylish album that in its variety sounds to me like a tenth generation descendant of the Beatmasters' *Anywayawanna* (someone reissue that, please!), especially on tracks like *Sex Murder Party*, combined with a techno crispness that reminded me of Inner City's marvellous debut album, all those years ago. There are twenty-six tracks in total, although seven are (brief) interludes. Highlights include "Momentz" featuring a turbo-charged De La Soul, "Ascension", with an angry Vince

Staples, and "Charger", in which Grace Jones slowly uncurls, regal, like an aural version of the Alien queen. "Provocative!" It's a joy that this song exists in the world. Apparently Grace Jones was in the studio for hours improvising her lyrics, and if there's a four hour version of this track I'd love to hear it. It also features 2D at his most delightfully feeble. Conversely, "Andromeda" features one of 2D's strongest vocal performances, on a track that could almost have been drawn from the Pet Shop Boys' sleek and groovy work with Stuart Price. "Submission" contrasts Kelela's gorgeous vocals with Danny Brown's hyperactive cartoon rap in a way that seems inexplicably perfect. "We Got the Power" is bottled inspiration, just when we all need it. The deluxe edition (surely the version most people will want) adds six tracks (one of them an interlude) to the twenty on the standard version, including another of the very best songs, "Out of Body", a herky-jerky dance number featuring Kilo Kish. The album is unpredictable but consistent, every song a novelty, full of weird noises and unexpected movements, with a multiplicity of voices woven into a whole by virtue of a consistently funky, tight sound. *Stephen Theaker* ★★★★☆

Television

Iron Fist, Season 1, by Scott Buck and chums (Marvel/Netflix)

Joy (Jessica Stroup) and Ward Meachum (Tom Pelphrey) are the siblings who run the immense multinational Rand Corporation, which was founded by Wendell Rand (who died with his family in a plane crash) and their unpleasant father (David Wenham), who died of cancer. A problem presents itself: a homeless man (Finn Jones) turns up at their building, claiming to be Danny Rand, son of their father's partner, and an old friend of theirs. If it is Danny Rand, he would own 51% of their company. At first they don't believe him, to the extent that they throw him out without asking a handful of obvious questions that could have easily confirmed his identity.

However, it soon becomes clear that he is really Danny Rand, and here they have a stroke of good fortune: he's a complete idiot who believes everything he is told, happily tells psychiatric doctors about his time in the mythical kingdom of K'un Lun, and is incapable of putting together the simplest clues as to what is really going on. Less fortunately for them, he begins to acquire capable and sensible allies: Colleen Wing (Jessica Henwick), a karate instructor who will help him fight, Claire Temple (Rosario Dawson, reprising her role from all the previous Netflix/Marvel shows), a nurse who will help him heal, and Jeri Hogarth (from *Jessica Jones*; Carrie-Anne Moss), a lawyer who will help him get his company back.

Very occasionally he uses the martial arts skills that he acquired during his absence (though he's very bad at knocking people out), and even more rarely he uses his special power, a glowing fist that can punch through anything. Joy and Ward don't seem that bright either, since Danny Rand doesn't really care about money, owning a company, or running a company; he only gets mired in that stuff in order to establish his identity and reclaim his name.

And so we get a show that spends masses of its time worrying about which of the repellant Meachums or their rivals (including the manipulative Madame Gao, played by Wai Ching Ho) is truly in charge of their company, while the titular character scowls his way through every scene and scampers around like a silly puppy at their beck and call. Viewers know that he has had a difficult time of it – the plane crash and subsequent years of apparently abusive training have left him suffering from post-traumatic stress disorder – and he has not lived in the modern world, but it's still hard to forgive his lack of regard for women's boundaries in the early episodes (he breaks into the homes of both Joy and Colleen) and the way that he constantly acts like a colossal jerk. It's hard to understand why Colleen Wing comes to like him so much, but thank goodness she does, because the programme would be much less watchable without her likeable and energetic presence. It picks up later as mysterious men Bakuto (Ramon Rodriguez) and Davos (Sacha Dawan) come to the fore, and with the latter there are even a few moments of much-needed comedy, but this still goes down as the least of the Netflix Marvel shows so far.

It was criticised before release by people who wished Danny had been played by an Asian actor. You can understand why they felt that way, but it would have been a completely different show: this is all about a rich white guy who is the first outsider to acquire the Iron Fist power, to the great resentment of those locals who thought it was their birthright. What harms the programme more is the actor's lack of martial arts skills. Season two could be better. It needs Danny to be a bit less one note in his reactions, it needs an antagonist who is in direct conflict with Danny rather than ambivalent towards him, and most importantly it needs much better fight scenes. The pace is no faster than season one of *Daredevil*, but in *Daredevil* the fights are worth the wait. In a show specifically about a martial arts master, the fight scenes need to be outstanding. *Stephen Theaker* ★★★☆☆

Legion, Season 1, by Noah Hawley and chums (FX)

It's astonishing that after creating season two of *Fargo*, probably my favourite programme of last year, Noah Hawley went straight on to creating this remarkable show, bringing Jean Smart and Rachel Keller with him. Some viewers took strongly against the slight science fiction elements of *Fargo*, but no complaints here since this is set in the X-Men universe. When exactly it is set has been a talking point, since of the X-Men films its design looks most like *X-Men: First Class*, set during the Cuban missile crisis, and the technology seems quite retro. Eventually an adult character, Ptonomy Wallace (Jeremie Harris), mentions hearing 99 Red Balloons on the radio when he was five years old. So my guess is that this is taking place in the

present day, or slightly in the future when the wheels of retro fashion have rotated once again.

There is another possibility, that we can't trust anything on screen, that this is how our protagonist sees the world. As in the comic which clearly inspired the show, *X-Men: Legacy* (reviewed in TQF59), our protagonist is David Haller (Dan Stevens, so good in *The Guest*), son of a powerful mutant, with a head full of powers. In the comic, the powers are his, each of his separate personalities having a different ability (like Crazy Jane of the Doom Patrol), and the powers activate either when he gets control of the split personality, or when the split personality gets control of his body. Things aren't so straightforward (if that's the word) in the programme. David is seen wielding immense power in moments of great stress, but whether the powers are his to control is unclear. He's been brought up to think that he is mentally ill, and he has been institutionalized ever since a particularly low point in his life. But at the institution he meets Syd Barrett, played by Keller, and their tentative, sweet romance will lead him out of the institution and into the middle of a war between mutants led by Dr Melanie Bird (Smart) and a mysterious, militaristic governmental department, while trying to cope with his burgeoning powers and mental health problems – if that indeed is what they are. Not everyone thinks so.

In the world of superhero adaptations, this programme stands apart. Much as I enjoy *The Flash* and *Supergirl*, no one would consider them a work of art, and that's what *Legion* is. Visually it is astounding, as stylish as the work of Mike Allred or Jack Kirby. It is probably the most self-indulgent programme I've seen this side of *Hannibal*, but I think it is exactly the programme it wants to be, and it trusts the viewer to go along for the ride – or perhaps trip would be a better word.

It is absolutely terrifying in places (what's that at the edge of David's memories?), but funny in others, and the experienced cast handle every turn of mood with aplomb. It reminded me at times of Patrick (H) Willem's short film, *What if Wes Anderson Directed X-Men?*, and I loved that about it. The words "best television ever" were uttered in our living room during the penultimate episode. Between this, *Dirk Gently* and *Preacher* it really does feel like they are making television programmes specifically for me these days. I hope other people are enjoying them too so I get plenty more of the same. *Stephen Theaker* ★★★★★

Notes

Also Received, But Not Yet Reviewed
Notes by Stephen Theaker

Aberrant, by Marek Šindelka (Twisted Spoon Press). A debut novel, described as "a heady concoction of crime story, horror story (inspired by the Japanese tradition of kaidan), ecological revenge fantasy, and Siberian shamanism".

Amatka, by Karin Tidbeck (Vintage). The debut novel by the author of *Jagganath*, an excellent collection of short stories, and this is very good too. Sorry my review wasn't ready for this issue. "Vanja, an information assistant, is sent from her home city of Essre to the austere, wintry colony of Amatka with an assignment to collect intelligence for the government. Immediately she feels that something strange is going on: people act oddly in Amatka, and citizens are monitored for signs of subversion."

Avengers of the Moon, by Allen Steele (Tor). A reboot of Captain Future, the Edmond Hamilton character: "Curt Newton has spent most of his life hidden from the rest of humankind, being raised by a robot, an android, and the disembodied brain of a renowned scientist. This unlikely trio of guardians has kept his existence a closely guarded secret after the murder of Curt's parents."

The Book Club, by Alan Baxter (PS Publishing). "Jason Wilkes's life takes a turn for the worse when his wife fails to come home from her book club."

The Face in the Shadows, by Iman Eyitayo (Plumes Solidaires). "This is a world where twins are not allowed to live. Seventeen-year-old Aluna lives in the shadows. She's a pariah. She was born a twin; but since the Lord Regent has arrived in Iriah to reign as a tyrant, twins have no right to live. However, when she breaks an ancient law by accident, thus reviving a conflict with the neighboring kingdom, she finds herself being everyone's main focus."

9 Tales of Raffalon, by Matthew Hughes (Matthew Hughes). A collection of short stories from one of my favourite writers.

People of the Sun, by Jason Parent (Sinister Grin Press). "All life comes from the sun. Sometimes, death comes with it. Filled with hope and compelled by fear, four would-be heroes are driven from their home planet in a desperate bid to save their civilization from extinction. But survival takes on a whole new meaning when a malfunction sends their ship plummeting toward Earth."

Red Snow, by Ian MacLeod (PS Publishing). "In the aftermath of the last great battle of the American Civil War, a disillusioned Union medic stumbles across a strange figure picking amid the corpses, and his life is changed forever..."

Sirens, by Simon Messingham (Derelict Space Sheep). "Without warning, without explanation, two hundred human beings on Earth simultaneously gained a new mental ability that would alter the planet forever. They called the power The Glamour and its recipients Sirens." The first original novel by the writer of several Doctor Who tie-ins.

Twin Peaks: Fire Walk with Me, by Maura McHugh (PS Publishing). Non-fiction book about the brilliant box-office flop, by a contributor to TQF35.

Void Star, by Zachary Mason (Jonathan Cape). The "mind-bending follow-up to [the author's] bestselling debut *The Lost Books of the Odyssey*".

Wasteland, by Malicious Wonderland (Soundcloud). A "dark ambient/industrial project" from Michigan. Listen at https://maliciouswonderland. bandcamp.com/album/wasteland.

We Are the Martians: The Legacy of Nigel Kneale, by Neil Snowden (ed.) (PS Publishing). Rescued from the collapse of Spectral Press.

Whisky, by Pinkberry (self-published). "Let's just be clear, talking to a girl is not the easiest thing in the world ... and if [Joe] is rejected, that could very well result in the total annihilation of our planet." A short story in ebook form, a "light contemporary romance".

You Will Grow Into Them, by Malcolm Devlin (Unsung Stories). A short story collection from a reliably interesting publisher. "Childhood anxieties manifest as debased and degraded doppelgängers, fungal blooms are harvested from the backs of dancers and lycanthropes become new social pariahs. The demons we carry inside us are very real indeed, but *You Will Grow Into Them*."

About TQF

Copyright

Website: www.theakersquarterly.blogspot.com

Email: theakersquarterlyfiction@gmail.com

Lulu Store: www.lulu.com/silveragebooks

Feedbooks: www.feedbooks.com/userbooks/tag/tqf

Submissions: Submissions are very welcome! See website for guidelines and terms and reading periods.

Advertising: We welcome ad swaps with small press publishers and other creative types, and we'll run free ads for relevant new projects from former contributors.

Sending material for review: We are happy to look at anything that's fantasy-related. We prefer to receive books for review in epub or mobi format, and comics in pdf or via Comixology. Feel free to send ebooks without querying first, but it's fair to warn you that we've only reviewed about 15% of items received since 2011, and even then that's often been stuff we've actively requested from places like NetGalley.

Mission statement: The primary goal of *Theaker's Quarterly Fiction* is to keep going. If you're wondering why we do something a particular way, our primary goal is probably why.

Copyright and legal: All works are copyright the respective authors, who have assumed all responsibility for any legal problems arising from publication of their material. Other material copyright Stephen Theaker and John Greenwood.

Published in Theaker's Paperback Library during September 2017.

Other Publications

Theaker's Quarterly Fiction
Stephen Theaker (ed.) *(#1–54, 56–57, 59)*
John Greenwood (ed.) *(#9–54, 56–57, 59)*
Douglas J. Ogurek (ed.) *(#58: Unsplatterpunk!)*
Howard Watts (ed.) *(#55)*

The Conan Doyle Weirdbook (ed.)
The Adventures of Roderick Langham
Rafe McGregor

Space University Trent: Hyperparasite
Walt Brunston

There Are Now a Billion Flowers
The Hatchling (forthcoming)
John Greenwood

The Mercury Annual
Pilgrims at the White Horizon
Michael Wyndham Thomas

Professor Challenger in Space
Quiet, the Tin Can Brains Are Hunting!
The Fear Man
His Nerves Extruded
The Doom That Came to Sea Base Delta

The Day the Moon Wept Blood
Stephen Theaker

Five Forgotten Stories
John Hall

Elephant
Harsh Grewal

Elsewhere
Steven Gilligan

New Words #1–4
John Greenwood, Steven Gilligan
and Stephen Theaker (eds)

Forthcoming Attractions

Expect **Theaker's Quarterly Fiction #61** in
September. We were open to fiction submissions for it
from 1 July 2017 to 31 August 2017.

We won't open to fiction subs for TQF62 (currently
planned to be a retro all-Theaker issue) but we will
open for TQF63 (the second Unsplatterpunk special)
from 1 October 2017 to 28 February 2017.

Our blog can be read here:
www.theakersquarterly.blogspot.com

Stephen tweets every few days or so at:
www.twitter.com/Rolnikov

The zine has its own Twitter account too:
www.twitter.com/TheakersQrtly

Our email address is:
theakersquarterlyfiction@gmail.com

If you've enjoyed this issue, and especially if you haven't, please consider giving it a rating on Goodreads, or LibraryThing, or wherever you keep track of your books. We don't need to sell any copies to keep going, so that's not a concern: it's just nice to know you're out there!